# DEATH
# & taxes

Robert Thompson

Cover and book design by Hailey Beazer
Keokee :: media + marketing in Sandpoint, Idaho

Printed in the United States of America

ISBN 978-1-7325667-0-5

Published by:
Robert Thompson
Sandpoint, Idaho

## Author's Note

All characters depicted herein are purely fictional. Any similarity to a real person is coincidental. There is no plot within the government to systematically extort and steal millions of dollars so far as I know. The campaign to abolish the income tax, and the individuals, organizations, committees, or other groups pushing that idea are not real. I made them up.

# Contents

# Preface

For much of the 20th Century and on into the 21st, public sector scandals have all too often occurred and are luridly reported. The object of these errant government officials is to misuse their authority to gain politically, financially and indulge themselves personally.

At the presidential level, we have seen LBJ's falsehoods regarding the Gulf of Tonkin attacks, one of which was completely fabricated to push the U.S. into the Vietnam War. Tricky Dick lied about Watergate, which ultimately forced Nixon from office. Ronald Reagan's Iran Contra was an attempt to bypass Congress with respect to funding a rebel group in Nicaragua and of course who can forget Slick Willie Clinton who lied about having sexual encounters in the Oval Office with a young female intern. Bush 43 used mythical weapons of mass destruction as reason to invade Iraq. There were no such weapons. Under Obama, the IRS was turned loose on groups who, it was feared, opposed the president's domestic policies.

These episodes are history. What this story is about is the unfettered power of the IRS and other government agencies have over your wallet and your freedom. The plot revolves around citizen tax reformers pushing for big changes. Their efforts are decidedly unappreciated by the government and the deadly battle is on.

While this is fiction, it is not hard to imagine it happening.


Conspiratorially Yours,

Robert Thompson

The fresh salt air and quiet beauty of Nantucket loosened Anderson Barton's anxious thoughts as he jogged along the road on his early morning run. It was chilly, with a brisk, bracing wind. Not the implacable cold of a Northeast coastline winter but not yet warm, as it would be soon, when thousands of tourists would flow off the ferries and onto the island, jostling the outnumbered year-rounders who nevertheless acknowledge that the visitors are their economic lifeblood.

He didn't mind the chill. He was beginning to sweat from pushing his mid-60s body into his familiar morning regimen. Later, after the run, he and Mary, his wife, would relax over breakfast at the family's historic cedar plank summer cottage. Then he would talk with Mary, and she would help him unravel his worries and fears. She is his love, his strong partner; his refuge for nearly 40 years.

Last night's dinner with her at their favorite Club Car restaurant had started to help back off the growing unease that Barton felt since he had agreed almost a year earlier to lead one of the world's most discredited bureaucracies. For the good of the country, he had told himself at the time. "What was I thinking?" he mused now. He had left behind his lucrative Washington, D.C., law firm of Palmer, Norman and Barton, with its political muscle and prestigious clients. He certainly had nothing to prove by taking on this late-in-life challenge. Child of a prominent Boston family and a Harvard Law grad, Barton had navigated the worlds of business and politics for decades with ease and considerable success. He even looked the part of a power elite, 6-foot-1, fit, only slightly gray at the temples and easily mistaken for a man 10 years younger.

He had flown into Nantucket Memorial Airport from D.C. the day before, leaving behind a daunting mess. Last year, the president had asked him to take charge of the besieged Internal Revenue Service. The administration's intent was opaque, to say the least. Whiffs of criminal activity inside the agency had surfaced and the administration knew that certain investigators were close to figuring out what was going on. This would not do! The implied message to Barton had been to make this nascent problem go away and he'd be well rewarded with some kind of career-capping victory lap after the looming election.

He and Mary already had talked after dinner last night. She was worried. He knew she had reason to be. He hadn't assumed the IRS commissioner role to help the administration cover up in the face of a hostile opposition-party Congress. He actually intended to fix whatever problems he found. The president and Barton's boss at the Treasury had other ideas. Close to his first anniversary on the job, there he was on the Hill, testifying at the Subcommittee of Taxation and IRS Oversight.

As he jogged down the road to the faint cries of sea birds, he pictured the hard glint in the eyes of his questioners. They had sensed his intent to take real action within the agency. Their focus had sharpened. The committee chairman had begun to demand names, dates, details. Barton had demurred at the public hearing, instead offering to produce information in a closed session. The chairman agreed, adjourned the meeting and set a date for three weeks hence.

Barton knew as he walked out of the hearing that he had to take refuge at the cottage, which all his life had been a place apart from the cares and cruelties of the world. He needed Nantucket at least for a few days until he could regain his resolve and prepare for what surely would become a national scandal.

"Do you know what you're doing?" Mary had asked last night after he had thrown his overnight bag in the corner of the hallway and settled next to her on the couch. He patted their dog, Douglas, a Wirehaired Pointing Griffon, who was sprawled at his feet, giving himself a moment to think before he answered.

"Yes and no," he said. "I guess I could say I'm trying to be noble. But the truth is I'm just pissed off."

Mary startled. She wasn't used to seeing her calm, thoughtful mate so openly riled. Even when their kids were little, loud and combative, he had maintained a maddening detachment while her mom-voice soared and her patience evaporated. She and Andy both were high-powered professionals, but all her negotiating skills would disappear in the face of fierce sibling rivalry. Not Andy, though. He would quietly find a way to divert their attention to a game or other activity. She already knew that feint would not work well on Congress. She had caught just enough evening news coverage of the hearing to know how serious a turn things had taken.

"The administration told me to stonewall," he said. "They intend to give those attack dogs in Congress nothing."

Mary shook her head. "That's not going to work," she said. "Don't they even know how to run a decent cover-up? Find somebody to shove under the bus, apologize and swear you didn't know about his transgressions, then drag our feet until the media and the public lose interest."

He chuckled for the first time in days. "You're assuming the White House knows what it''s doing. They assume that handing me a script and dictating how I should handle the mess will make everything OK."

"Well," she answered, "I am not sure spilling your guts to Congress is going to go over too well at the IRS or anyplace else, for that matter. I want you to come out of this OK. Please be careful."

"I'll try, I'm kind of on my own here. But I'll find a way."

Going into the job, he had assumed he would find the usual scratch-each-other's-backs tax break favors being done on behalf of big campaign donors. Depressing and immoral, certainly enough to anger the middle-class taxpayer if publicly disclosed, but probably just inside the lines of Byzantine tax laws. One of his more humanist law partners often said that tax law was like the Bible – look long enough and you'd find a passage enabling your actions. But what Barton had found as he listened, watched and deduced over the months was much more ominous. Corruption seemed to have seeped deep into the bureaucracy at the IRS's Constitution Avenue headquarters, governmental thievery approaching that of the world's most infamous plutocracies.

He couldn't shake these thoughts. Usually his morning jog cleared out negativity. Now flashes of the hearing, his wife's worried face, and images of turmoil to come tumbled in his mind. Fragmented, anxiety-driven chaos. "Breathe! You can get through this!" he told himself.

He didn't feel pain as the vehicle's front bumper lifted him – just a flash of wonder at why he was airborne. Strange … no pain! He did not realize that his spine already had snapped, so the agony of shattered bones could not be conveyed to his brain. He landed face-up by the side of the road, still conscious. "Mary will worry … no breakfast together after she wakes." A Cooper's hawk circled high above searching for prey.

Having fulfilled its mission, the vehicle quickly disappeared down the road and into the back of a waiting van. It had been a clean hit. No witnesses. The driver soon would confirm to his masters: commissioner Barton was dead.


It had been a while and the dog still watched for him at the cottage. With their sons on either side of her, Mary had said goodbye to her husband at Prospect Hill Cemetery, watching as his coffin was lowered into its place in the family plot. She was numb at the funeral. The anger and suspicion came later. Soon she would close the Nantucket house and return to Washington. She would find out why her husband had been left to die on a sparsely traveled road, on an island that had gone for years without a pedestrian fatality. Fueling her rage was the president's seeming indifference to Barton's death. Other Washington friends had written or called. Some made it to the funeral. Not a personal word from the president and only a perfunctory note from the Treasury secretary.

# Chapter 2

Gordon "Mac" Macdonald never thought of himself as a reformer of any kind, much less a fiscal policy or tax reformer. His fate, to the contrary, was sealed with a phone call, which amounted to a summons to duty from his uncle.

A 45-year-old management consultant based in Los Angeles, Mac was born into a loving family torn apart by the Vietnam War. His dad, John Macdonald, whom he remembered through the eyes of a five-year-old, was shot down and killed on a mission near the end of the war. Young Mac and his mother, Martha, were left on their own.

In New York City for a number of days to meet with one of his firm's biggest clients, Mac was finally flying home to L.A. His 6-foot frame barely folded into the plane seat. At least it was on the aisle.

The urgent call from his uncle triggered memories of his early life because Uncle Bob was such an omnipotent force as the adult male figure, mentor and steady presence for 30 years.

His actual memories of his father, John, were scant. But he knew his father from the family stories relayed by his mother and a few more from Uncle Bob. His mom spoke fondly of their college days at USC and remembered well the early years of marriage to a well turned out U.S. Navy pilot. Their time at Miramar Naval Air Station in San Diego was an exciting start to their life together. Five years later, their life together was ended tragically by the war.

After six years, Martha, as attractive as ever, had enough of being a widow. She married a man 10 years her senior, a divorced high-powered litigator. His law practice pushed him into the social fast lane. That was OK with mother Martha – she reveled in it.

By this time, Mac was 11 years old and still hurting from his dad's untimely death. From the get-go, he was not wild about his new step-father. By age 13, Mac and the new Lion King were in open warfare. Martha was unable to intervene effectively.

It wasn't a case of Martha not caring about her son - she cared a lot and she proved it with over a decade of nurturing care. It was about her capacity to deal with a no-win situation. The new Lion King had set about to drive out the progeny of his predecessor.

It was then that his Uncle Bob stepped in big. The aggrieved young Mac had a new home. They were not strangers, but both had a lot to learn about the new living arrangement. Uncle Bob was a bachelor with a social life and deeply involved in the running of his construction company. He was not trained to be a parent, but was a quick learner and his fierce family loyalty prevailed.

Before too long, young Mac realized he was again the center of attention. His survival skills were honed as he learned laundry, dish-washing, entry-level cooking and of course trash removal. In his new role as parent, Robert Macdonald was also a stern task master when it came to school work.

Uncle Bob was anxious and angry about the direction of the national economy. Garrulous, occasionally profane, generous to friends and family, Mac's uncle was a contrarian unimpressed by arbitrary au-thority. He lived in a blue state, but his politics were decidedly not left-leaning - nor were they classically conservative. He was independent in the true sense of the word. He had little regard for politicians and a special distrust for the corrupt and corrosive federal tax code. Yes, Mac thought, his uncle was never subtle about what was on his mind.

The long flight had made Mac ever more eager to see his girlfriend, Sarah Ferguson, who was meeting him at LAX. A lithe, athletic and in-tensely focused security professional, brown-haired, pretty Sarah, was the first woman in Mac's life he considered his soulmate. They'd met on a scuba diving boat trip off the California coast four years earlier and almost immediately had settled into a passionate and monogamous relationship, well spiced with humor and only the occasional spat. They were a great match.

As the plane descended on approach for landing and the sprawl of L.A. came into sight, Mac thought about the intense tone his uncle took in their last conversation.

"It sounds like our government money situation is dire," Uncle Bob had said. "Treasury will try to B.S. Congress and push for raising the debt limit and hope to keep things going. It's too close to the election, so no real reform is possible at this time."

"We've heard it all before. The news will be largely ignored," replied Mac.

"Yes, exactly," Uncle Bob answered. "I'm having a few people over to my home on Sunday around noon. Come along and I think you'll find it interesting and be sure to invite Sarah."

"I'll be there," Mac answered.

On Sunday, Mac and Sarah drove across town to Uncle Bob's home to see what the peppery non-conformist was up to. When they arrived, Bob greeted them and introduced a handful of others, all, like their host, in or near their 60s and similarly successful in business, public service or philanthropy. Lunch was spread in the dining area of the spacious home as the guests mingled and bemoaned the state of the country.

"Who are these guys?" Sarah whispered to Mac. "They all seem to be plenty wealthy and not panicked at all by the crisis in Washington."

"I have no clue," Mac said. "I guess we listen and learn."

The lunch chatter touched on the Sunday morning talk shows. Mark Nelson, Uncle Bob's college friend, was particularly critical of media peers – he was a Washington, D.C., correspondent for the Los Angeles Times. "In my 25 years covering D.C., the quality of critical investigative reporting has never been weaker. The media's been absorbed into the permanent political class. We're supposed to be the watchdogs, not part of the governmental machine."

"What do you make of the IRS guy's death?" asked Robert Macdonald.

"Don't know much, but it's sure a coincidence that he gets run down right before he was scheduled to testify in a closed congressional hearing."

Sarah drifted away from Mac after a while and sought out the only other woman at the gathering. Maggie McFarland, a 60-year-old former Superior Court judge, was curious about Sarah, easily the youngest person at the gathering.

"Tell me about yourself," Maggie said.

"Born and raised in Missoula, Montana, but came to California to go to UC Berkeley, I loved California so much I never left," said Sarah.

"I'll bet it was culture shock at first!" said Maggie.

"No kidding," Sarah said, laughing. "It was kind of hard focusing on math and computer science in the middle of that gigantic, sometimes raucous place! Especially for a country girl. But when I found my way to Southern California, I fell in love. Where else can you see the surf off Santa Monica beach and be on a ski run near Big Bear two or three hours later?"

Maggie smiled. "I'll bet you miss Montana sometimes though - especially when you're stuck in a traffic jam. Any siblings?"

"One brother. He did a stint in the Marines then went back home to Montana. He's not as fond of big cities as I am," answered Sarah.

"So what do you do?" asked Maggie.

"It's going to bore you," Sarah warned. "I work for South Bay Security, an offshoot of an aerospace firm. It conducted highly classified surveillance of the USSR until the early '90s, then got spun off. Now we provide a variety of security services."

"Fascinating!"

"Well, sometimes … I'm mostly involved with data security, corporate and personal. That can be tedious or kind of interesting, depending on the day."

Across the lunch table, one of the quieter members of the group, banker John Reed, broke his silence, homing in on Mac.

"What do you make of this Treasury debacle?" he asked.

"People will get scared and make a run for gold, foreign currency – anything they think will protect their wealth."

"Longer term?"

Before Mac could answer, Martin Prescott, former governor of the Federal Reserve, broke in saying, "Our country is a debt zombie! We're drowning in debt and we just keep borrowing. We're stalled – a bad tax system and the debt are barriers to growth and all the government does is 'extend and pretend.'" He shook his head in disgust.

As lunch wound down, Uncle Bob got Mac aside and asked him to meet again on Monday. On the drive home, Mac and Sarah still were wondering what the meeting really was about.

"I got the feeling we were being interviewed for jobs," she said. "Tell me more about your uncle."

"USC grad, then the Army and a tour in Vietnam two years before my dad. I think he feels it deeply that he survived and my dad didn't. They both were 1950s kind of guys, traditional as they come, even though they were baby boomers. Lots of their friends were involved in the anti-war movement in the '60s. Not them. After my dad died, Uncle Bob took over helping raise me."

She heard a catch in his voice and realized for the first time how much he loved his uncle. She gently redirected the conversation. "He never married?"

"Never, although there were plenty of women in his life. He always seemed to be too busy to settle down. Some would say he pulled off every guy's dream – relationships with hot women involving great sex and no long-term commitments."

"Uh huh, OK smartass, have you met any of his ladies?"

"Sure and so have you."

Sarah thought for a minute. "Maggie?"

"Yep. Before Maggie was a judge, she did legal work for Uncle Bob and they were an item for a couple of years."

Sarah grew pensive and Mac sensed there was something coming his way.

"How about you, Mr. Mac? Are you following in your uncle's footsteps?"

Suddenly they were in serious territory. He tried to keep the tone light.

"Do you mean am I a confirmed bachelor?" he asked with a smile.

"I mean to ask, what is our future? We've both had other relationships. Is this the one we want to keep?"

"You are the last to arrive and still the first one here. I love you," Mac said, "And if you let me, I'll be yours for keeps."

As they approached the driveway of their condo, Sarah smiled and said, "Maybe – how about a test drive before I buy the car?"

Into the house they went. It was an early night and a long night.

# Chapter 3

As Mac arrived at his uncle's house, Monday as invited, he sensed that he was about to be recruited for some sort of task.

Quick to the point, Uncle Bob asked, "How much do you know or even care about federal tax policy and practices? Is it too complicated? Too boring? Well, I wouldn't be surprised if that is the truth."

Somewhat taken aback by his uncle's aggressive greeting, Mac replied, "Are you pissed at me?"

Uncle Bob dialed it down a notch and said, "Have some coffee and I'll explain what's on my mind. I'm talking about the IRS. We, as a nation, are getting screwed royally by our federal government. Crony capitalism is the dirty deed and the IRS is the tool by which we are penetrated."

"That's kind of a crude way to put it, don't you think?" asked Mac.

"So what? Are we supposed to be polite about it?" answered Uncle Bob.

"From that opening, I suspect you have some ideas on how to fix it. Proceed, I'm all ears," said Mac.

"Damn straight I do!" Uncle Bob said, picking up steam.

"Even the Ivy League types are catching on. Graduates who make decisions as to where to establish or expand their businesses pick foreign locations most of the time. They cite our political system which is in the crapper from corruption, our tax code which is also a product of corruption, regulations, many ill–conceived, and hiring and firing as inflexible. Only our lawyers think we have a good legal system.

"Our income tax system is killing us. It's too expensive, harms productivity and is unfair. Combine that with overspending by Congress and it's easy to see why we are going broke!"

As Mac thought it over, Uncle Bob continued: "Let me fill you in, Mac, on how I got started on this tax issue. The money problem at the federal level most recently intensified in 1960. What was that you ask? You were not even born! It was the end of the Eisenhower presidency, which had some fiscal discipline and decent capital spending goals. Then came an endless parade of U.S. government deficits to fund wars and social programs on the cuff.

"Kennedy was not in office long enough to really count, but his successor LBJ surely was. The Great Society and the Vietnam War deficit spending started the ball rolling. No administration since Eisenhower, except a tiny bit of Clinton, who probably did it unintentionally, has conducted proper financial management.

"The election of 2008 was proof positive that our political system is in the tank. The previous administrations had left a piss-poor fiscal and monetary situation and the U.S. elected a rank amateur to fix it. At this time, the federal, state and local governments spend about half of the gross domestic product, which requires confiscatory levels of taxation and more borrowing.

"As bad as the consequence for poor economic growth works out for most citizens, it is small potatoes compared to what we have lost worldwide," said Uncle Bob.

"What are you talking about?" asked Mac. "The U.S. is the largest economy in the world."

"For the moment," replied Uncle Bob, "But that won't last long as we concede military, economic and political power to others.

"Following World War II, the U.S. was the de facto successor to the European, mostly British, empires. We were the only major country that was not severely damaged in its homeland and over 70 percent of the world's capital was held in the U.S. These circumstances combined to make this country in charge of world order.

"As we discovered, that position of top dog in the world is quite profitable. The U.S. as a whole prospered and in particular a large middle class was created. Our country was able to utilize that immense pool of capital to the world's benefit," said Uncle Bob.

"So what? That was then and this is now. Is there a point to this little history lesson?" asked a rather exasperated Mac.

Uncle Bob answered, "I'm glad you asked, my young student! We can do it again; we can become economically world dominant without a military conflict. We need convincing military power as a backstop, but the real weapon is money and banking. The key to obtaining that power is to abolish the income tax. If you don't tax capital and do provide a profitable environment, capital will flow to you. The U.S. will become again the dominant financial power of the world. The economy will grow gangbusters!"

"Hey! Hold it up a minute. Didn't the U.S. have sky-high income tax rates during the years following World War II? And then only five years later the Korean intervention began, again necessitating high income tax rates?" asked Mac.

"Very observant, Mac. The key to the post-war expansion was the presence of most of the world capital in the U.S. The availability of capital is what makes things go. So why was that capital here to begin with, you ask? The answer is, after tax yield, adjusted for risk, was higher in the U.S. compared to other areas. Risk; the key was risk. In other words, the physical destruction, economic, political and social conditions in much of the world outside the U.S. made investments relatively safe here.

"As Europe, Japan and other countries recovered, improved investment conditions attracted a fair amount of capital back. When risk is the same for a given income stream you are left with the variation in tax rates to account for capital flows.

"If you have any doubt about that, just look at the tax exempt municipal bond market compared to fully taxable bonds of the same credit quality and duration. The munis sell for higher prices and lower yield, because it's risk adjusted after tax rate of return that counts," said Uncle Bob.

"OK, for the sake of argument, assume the income tax is a poor system. Saying you are getting rid of the IRS and the income tax sounds like good fun, but what goes in their place? The government does need to collect tax revenue somehow," said Mac.

"You have just asked the most obvious question, but also the most difficult to explain to anyone but a tax expert. Even the tax lawyers and accountants will come down on opposing sides of what is the best tax system. Volumes have been written on the subject, but let me give you my answer and a few reasons why.

"A broad-based consumption tax is the best alternative to our present income tax system.

"Size matters; consumption in the U.S. is about 95 percent of personal income. Much personal income is not taxed for a variety of reasons; some good and some bad. It is possible to have a multiple level sales tax which would levy on manufacturers, wholesalers, retailers and service providers. Taxable consumption transactions would therefore apply to a larger dollar base and would have a lower tax rate as a result.

"Size matters again; everyone residing in the U.S. would pay some tax thus increasing the taxpayer base.

"For a size matters triple play, consider this: the tax revenue collected for the government's use would be adequate in amount and more predictable, thus greatly reducing the revenue deficits we now experience," said Uncle Bob.

"Who wins and who loses? Is not taxation a zero sum game?" asked Mac.

"Only if the size of the economy is static," Uncle Bob continued. "Growth in economic activity will help everyone to prosper.

"My next point is one that no one can contest. As citizens, our individual liberty, rights to property and the pursuit of happiness are all put at risk from the IRS. Their collection powers are the playbook for any aspiring dictator.

"As I have said, concentration of power anywhere in the government will lead to trouble and we have it in spades at the IRS.

"The need to intervene became obvious to a number of active business, professional, labor and government leaders after the 2008 elections. Several years ago, I was invited to attend an extended weekend retreat by my friend and former banker, John Reed. The group was an informal committee of 20 members and eight prospective members. The meeting was held at a fishing camp in western Montana, not far from Butte. The agenda was morning fly fishing, then public policy discussions in the afternoon and early evening.

"Two days into the event came the interesting part when the plan was put forth. We are going to attempt to eliminate the income tax. No other single government activity holds more sway over American citizens' lives than does the collection of income taxes. Even with the power they have, the IRS only collects 70 percent of taxes due under the tax code.

"Our major premise is that a large and prosperous middle class is a good thing, which depends upon economic growth and a system of meritocracy. As presently conducted, the income tax discourages rational economic activity and its collection corrupts government. It interferes with the development of a strong middle class. Our premise is that all will do better without the income tax. The social safety net will be left in place and improved."

"Excuse me, Uncle Bob, but this sounds quixotic. It is a visionary, but impractical proposal for reform," said Mac.

"Impractical in what way?" said Uncle Bob.

"Politics is a contact sport. The government has the upper hand. They will send men with guns if you don't comply with their rules. But more than that, it would be a tough sell to the public. The progressive tax rates are understandably popular with most taxpayers. Only the top 20 to 30 percent of income earners pay proportionately more in taxes than they earn in income," said Mac.

"It's true that a point of sale consumption tax would tax high earners a greater dollar amount, since they spend more, but it would be a lower percentage of their income compared to middle and low income earners. There is a way of adjusting for that regressive tax rate outcome.

"Studies have been conducted that demonstrate that a tax rate equalizer, sometimes referred to as a rebate, paid to every legal resident household in the U.S. according to size, would offset much of the regressive nature of the consumption tax, particularly at the lower income levels" said Uncle Bob.

"That seems a little nutty to me," replied Mac.

"Not really," said Uncle Bob, "If you set the base amount of the rebate, the government would pay to each and every legal household equal to 90 percent of the amount of consumption tax that would be paid by the lowest quartile of income earners, it would mean that the lowest income group would have a nearly net zero tax. For the next quartile, it would amount to about half of their consumption taxes. As you go up the income scale, the government tax rate equalizer payment would amount to a smaller percent of income, thus creating tax increases in dollar amounts, but at a lower rate as the base becomes larger. This is known as a digressive rate structure.

"Let's think about the issue of fairness in taxation. As a fighter pilot might say, this subject is target rich. It begins with who should pay, how much, and who gets to levy the tax.

"It's often observed that the ability to pay is paramount and therefore progressive income taxation is important. Others might add that benefits received are an equally important consideration.

"If progressive taxation is really important, then why is it so easily defeated by wealthy, high income corporations and individuals? There are two obvious reasons: The first reason is that income tax exemptions and special lower rates are routinely purchased from Congress. Secondly, sharply progressive income taxation is a poor idea to begin with. If its purpose is to adequately fund the government, it has failed. If it is attempting to redistribute income and wealth, it has failed. What it has succeeded at is blunting proper incentives in the economy.

"As to how much tax should be paid there are at least two main points: how much does the government really need in order to pay for its activities, and at some upper level, heavy taxes can harm the tax base.

"Who gets to levy the tax is also a two-part issue. We all know it is a legislative function. But that is just the beginning, particularly with the income tax. Special interests and political considerations have resulted in the majority of voters shifting the burden to the middle class and above, who actually pay most of the tax. This is fondly known as 'demand more from the government and tax the other guy to pay for it.' Our legislators heartily embrace this system, because it makes it easy to raise funds, get reelected and grow the government.

"I have read study after study on how to fix the problem of the stagnant economy, the decline of the middle class, and the futility of government efforts to be a net positive force. They all just nibble around the edges.

"The answer is startlingly obvious and simple. The only federal tax of adequate size that can be easily and fairly collected is a multiple level sales tax. In that fashion, everyone in the country pays the tax and receives the benefits. Abolish not only the income tax, but the class warfare and corruption that go along with it,"

"We are not the first to propose this general idea. Over a decade ago, there was introduced in the House of Representatives and the Senate, the Fair Tax Act of 2005. It never was passed into law, but it did bring up the subject," said Uncle Bob.

"How do you expect a group of 28 individuals, more or less, to affect this magnitude of change?" asked Mac.

"The business and labor organizations in the U.S. are going to see the international economic opportunities here," said Uncle Bob.

"So you propose to establish worldwide American domination through the use of capital?" asked Mac.

"You are spot-on, Mac! Said Uncle Bob. "In fact, the name of our Association is called The Capital Club."

"The Capital Club's governing authority is the committee, which is a political action committee. You and Sarah met some members at my home. There is a chairman and we are assembling a paid staff.

"The membership of the committee includes representatives of various businesses, labor unions and professionals from all representative areas of the country. The idea is to present the country's employers and workers with an action plan to preserve their business and jobs that within a few months will induce Congress to endorse the action. Every member of Congress has been, or will be, contacted by constituents that they already know.

"Don't forget, it is the government that has broken its covenant with the U.S. citizens. Financial promises can no longer be met. Without this magnitude of events, none of this effort to reform would stand a chance," said Uncle Bob.

"Even if I concede that the consumption tax is superior to the income tax, I don't see how that will help with the problems of poor quality government officials," Mac said. "Won't Congress continue to pass vaguely written legislation for which they are paid with campaign contributions and then lateral off the extortion opportunity to bureaucrats who write the rules?"

"You have to start somewhere," Uncle Bob replied. "Taking tax favors off the table will help a lot. A balanced budget requirement, with some specific exceptions, for every two-year cycle of the House of Representatives would also help. Maybe term limits of, say, six years for the House and 12 years for the Senate would cut down on incumbent fundraising."

"What do you intend to do about the financial chaos that is picking up steam as we speak?" said Mac.

"Stay out of harm's way as best we can," answered Uncle Bob.

"How?" said Mac.

"It's not an overstatement to say we saw it coming. This failure is years in the making. As late as 1998 to 2000, it seemed like our government would get it right. Economic growth had produced a budget surplus. A self-proclaimed conservative had been elected president. Then the attack of September 11th changed everything. Without the slightest effort to pay for it, the U.S. went to war once again, against a country that had little or nothing to do with the events of 9/11.

"In 2006 our political action committee was formed to raise funds for our efforts. Now it's a war chest. In 2008, the Association evolved to an action entity and at this time has extensive contacts with business, professional, labor and government individuals who agree with our cause," said Uncle Bob.

"What's been going on with the stock markets this morning?" asked Mac.

"The scene at the New York Stock Exchange has been frantic. Within minutes of the opening, the high frequency traders had kicked off the bust.

"The selloff is crushing stock prices. In the first hour, 15 percent of the market capitalization had been lost. Circuit breakers had been invoked to slow the trade, but nothing could really stop the capitulation of sellers. By day's end, you can expect another 15 percent of market prices will be lost.

"This free fall is approaching the 25 percent decline that occurred on Black Monday in the fall of 1987. Today's loss of 6,000 points on the Dow is a painful shock, but when you think about it, it will get worse by week's end. There will be no immediate Federal Reserve intervention, except to purchase some Treasury bills and other government-backed securities to help with liquidity. There will be no institutional support and therefore no real buyers - only sellers. The machine will seize up. Banks and other institutions will lose liquidity because the value of assets will rapidly shrink. The fractional banking system in reverse will screw up the entire economy," said Uncle Bob.

"And we are going to do what?" said Mac.

"We have in mind helping our government recover from its self-inflicted wounds.

"Our Capital Club offers a way out. It will not be business as usual. Our committee believes it has the contacts in Congress and the resources to create a new system whose power is returned to the American citizens," said Uncle Bob.

"I'm surprised you are willing to undertake this reform project – you've already won the game. What's in it for you?" asked Mac.

"The fact that the system has worked for me, giving me the opportunities for success I've had, leads me to insist that we must preserve and in some ways improve our American way of life. Allowing our public and private institutions to deteriorate the way they have is just plain sloppy. We ignore or tolerate seemingly small transgressions until they become large and as is the case today, quite harmful to citizens across the board. I guess you could say I feel a duty, especially when I am convinced that I see clearly at least one of the major problems and how to fix it," said Uncle Bob.

# Chapter 4

Josh Finn was an unlikely murder victim. Hailing from a well-to-do family in Los Angeles, he went east to D.C. by way of college at UCSB.

While at the university, he was on the political sidelines, enjoyed the abundant social life in Isla Vista, adjacent to Santa Barbara, and was a semi-serious student. As an econ major, his education spanned the liberal arts world and the more precise environment of economics. At 6-foot-3, he was well suited for competition on the crew team where he rowed for three years.

The Palmer, Norman and Barton firm was more than a law practice. As a premier lobbyist, it offered knowledge of government policy on energy, health care, taxes and everything in between. Finn was recruited from college to join their research staff.

"Welcome to D.C.," the intern manger said to the half-dozen new recruits assembled in a conference room, "Each of you please tell me why you are in our intern program."

When it was Josh's turn, he offered, "In school I was an econ major. It seems to me that every aspect of economic, social and business life is influenced by the federal government. So, here I am, hopefully close to the action."

After the orientation, Josh and Barry, a black kid from Harvard, were teamed up to do tax policy research. A few months in, it became apparent that Barry's skill and interest was in political organizing while Josh was fast becoming knowledgeable on tax policy. Barry left the firm and went into community organizing and a year later, Josh went to work for the House Ways and Means Committee.

A decade and a half into his work on the committee staff, he progressed to the position of the senior staff member to the Chairman of the House Ways and Means Committee. Josh was the traffic cop for anyone doing business on tax matters.

It is the Congressional Committee that must give birth to any serious tax legislation. And so it was that the proposal to substitute a broad-based consumption tax for the income tax as the main funding source for the federal government landed on Josh Finn's desk.

It was a bit of a radical notion in that it would leave many winners and losers in its wake. Early on in the campaign, the potential losers organized much more strongly than did those who would gain.

In the main, the biggest losers would be those organizations that paid dearly for income tax breaks such as participants in municipal bonds, REITS, oil and gas production and transportation and those who shift taxable income to low-tax offshore locations while leaving a large presence in the U.S.

Josh was feeling the heat from more than a few lobbyists. As he learned more, Josh began to favor the consumption tax idea. Efforts to change Josh's mind started with bribery and as his advocacy for tax change increased, the blackmail attempts began.

His sexual orientation was not widely known even though he had some selective contact with the gay community. Threatened with wide public exposure, Josh opted to "come out," thus negating the blackmail attempt. What next?

Several weeks after Josh's announcement, there was an altercation in a gay bar which spilled out into the street. Several persons were injured and one fatality occurred. The senior congressional staff member had been killed. The hate crime narrative kicked in, the media went wild and a senseless crime was lamented – except that it was not senseless at all!

Nobody is more adept at validating or debunking a D.C. conspiracy theory than the manager of a top lobbying firm. Carson Palmer has been at the helm from the beginning. He was one of the founders of the Palmer, Norman and Barton firm some 30 years ago.

Just as a three-legged step ladder will support a heavily laden carpenter, so too did the emergence of the three critical facts support the improbable IRS conspiracy theory.

To begin with, tax law changes that have a chance are met with resistance in proportion to the financial harm to be inflicted. The weapons are usually non-lethal. The drastic nature of the extinction of the IRS, it is being rumored, is the exception to the rule.

Next, the body count is mounting. Two major government figures have been killed who both were likely to take actions inimical to the survival of the IRS. Commissioner Barton and congressional aide Finn were killed on purpose, which screams conspiracy.

Mary Barton had advanced the ball up the field considerably when she met with Carson Palmer and disclosed what only she knew of her husband's information and his suspicions concerning the IRS. She might be easily dismissed as being biased in the matter of her husband's death, except for the fact that she was a D.C. insider with a long record of civic and professional involvement. Mary knew her husband was a threat to some in the IRS and that is why he was murdered. Josh Finn was likewise a threat to some in various government agencies if, as a result of his efforts and those of others, the IRS was abolished.

From that, it can conclusively be argued that it would be dangerous to oppose the IRS in the income tax abolition matter. There is no doubt at all that some type of organization within the government is committing murder.

# Chapter 5

Ed Dugan, a senior IRS audit supervisor, was realizing that a credible, building threat to the imperious IRS had caused a seismic shift in its strategy and tactics. Dugan had spent 35 years in the tax business and knew an incipient tax revolt when he saw one. He found himself questioning what would happen now that extortion, intimidation and bribery weren't enough? Physical violence, he thought.

Dugan was more than a sideline observer. He was in his early 60s and on the verge of retirement; he had a plan for life after the IRS. His final assignment was to conduct an audit of a relatively small consulting firm in Los Angeles, Gordon Macdonald and Associates. Dugan had requested this last assignment.

The name Macdonald rang a bell with Dugan because he became aware of the Capital Club's status as a PAC. The two Macdonalds had some interconnected businesses so that an audit of one would ensnare the other. That is if Dugan wanted it that way.

Dugan's rise through the ranks of government bureaucracy was average at best. More would have been expected taking into account that he came from an Irish middle-class family in Massachusetts and attained a degree in accounting from Boston College. For most of the 35 years, he was just a nine-to-five guy.

A come-to-Jesus moment occurred during his last two years of service. Married early and divorced late, Dugan had some financial ground to make up. He had caught a glimpse of a shadow union of government employees in the money laundering business. It was time to become entrepreneurial in the tradition of many who monetize their government experience upon retirement.

The Macdonald tax audit began – first the notification letter from the IRS and then an in-person visit.

In attendance were two from the IRS: Dugan, tall and bulky, and a relatively new frail-looking agent by the name of Weaver, and then Mac and his tax representative, Ackerman, who was also a rather large man.

Dugan and Weaver opened up with an outline of topics ranging from timing of income and expense recognition to backup data in support of deductions and so on. The meeting ended after two hours and as the IRS agents were on the way out, Dugan nodded to Mac and asked to speak with him briefly.

"What's on your mind, Mr. Dugan?" asked Mac.

"This will be my last assignment with the government. Confidentially for now, I have made arrangements to form a consulting organization which deals with the political aspects of federal taxation."

"Interesting," said Mac, "What prompted this idea?"

"It couldn't have escaped your attention that income tax policies and issues are increasingly intertwined with partisan politics. Maybe I can be helpful," said Dugan.

"Perhaps you can," said Mac, "Since we are speaking off the record, can I ask what is going on with the musical chairs act with the IRS commissioners? First a couple of years ago, the commissioner is laughed out of office because he used the dog ate his homework excuse for not producing required data and then the next guy gets run over and killed! Now we have his acting replacement who is only required to keep the seat warm until the election. This looks bad – even for the government."

"I can't really comment on the commissioners now, Mr. Macdonald. But I can say that it has always been, and most likely always will be, the upper level civil service administrators and congressional senior staff that run the show – and the show will go on," replied Dugan.

"You've got my interest and I would appreciate learning more. Please call me when you're available to proceed," said Mac.

"I will. By the way, years ago I was leading an audit team that dealt with your uncle, Robert Macdonald, when he was in the construction business. He may remember me. Please say hello for me," said Dugan.

Uncle Bob was on the line. "Mac, I want to invite you to lunch tomorrow. My place at noon."

Mac agreed and arrived at noon the next day.

"Have you considered joining our committee?" asked Uncle Bob.

"I have, but I'm not sure. It could be a futile effort, because big fiscal changes, even good ones, are difficult to come by," replied Mac.

"To be frank with you, I know getting rid of the federal income tax in favor of a consumption tax is a long shot at this time. However, as the economy worsens, the benefits of change will become more obvious," said Uncle Bob.

"I'll give it a try, based on your say-so," said Mac.

"There will be a meeting of the Association's committee tomorrow. I hope you can make it," said Uncle Bob.

"I can," answered Mac, "When and where?"

"One of our members has a place in Carmel Valley near Monterey. I'll pick you up at Santa Monica Airport and we'll fly up. He has a landing strip on his property."

"Who is this person?" asked Mac.

"James Townsend. He's a recently retired Air Force general and serves as our chairman," said Uncle Bob.

Changing the subject, Mac said, "By the way, I'm going through an IRS audit. The agent in charge says he did an audit on your construction business years ago. He said to say 'hello' to you."

"That wouldn't be Ed Dugan, would it?" asked Uncle Bob.

"Yes it is - what's his story?" asked Mac.

"The long and short of it was that I helped solve a problem for him and he did likewise for me," said Uncle Bob.

"I think he is looking for a return engagement," said Mac. "First he tells me this is his last job, because he is retiring, then he goes on to say he can be helpful with the politics which drives the IRS. Why tell me? I'm small potatoes. Do I have a problem with the IRS I don't know about?"

"Maybe I do," said Uncle Bob thoughtfully. "He didn't get the assignment to audit you by chance. Dugan must want to contact me and he chose to go through you to do it. Call him back to discuss some minor item in your audit and find out what he's up to. He may realize the Treasury problems will be a game changer."

"May I ask what the issues were, when you were back-scratching each other?" asked Mac.

"For him, it was a girlfriend that his wife found out about. Fortunately for Dugan, Macdonald Construction had a position available that called for extensive travel. The girlfriend took the job and became the former girlfriend. Even with that, Dugan's wife divorced him a couple of years later.

"On my side, I had some labor union problems that required some expenditures and their true nature would have been a problem, if known. Dugan fixed it," said Uncle Bob.

# Chapter 6

After takeoff from Santa Monica, Uncle Bob came clean with Mac, disclosing that he had proposed Mac as president of the Capital Club. Mac was naturally surprised and more than a bit mystified.

"Why me?" asked Mac. "I'm not experienced in tax matters!"

"That and the fact that you are too young to know better," Uncle Bob quipped. "Seriously, we need young energetic talent. Your business experience is strong and you will have available all the technical backup you need."

Mac realized his uncle really wanted this from him and that there were more than a few due bills accumulated over the years of their relationship.

The Capital Club's committee, now numbering 28, was assembled. Mac and Uncle Bob arrived just before noon as lunch was being served.

Introductions were made, even though most of the members were previously well acquainted. Mac was the only non-member in attendance. It seemed as if the introductions were for Mac's benefit only.

First up was a progress report on the recruitment of associates. In order to be an associate, a person must have authority or influence over a significant aspect of American business, labor, political, law, public safety, health and other professional activities.

As the reports went on, Mac became impressed at the magnitude and quality of those mentioned. Several of his consulting clients were included in this group.

Next up was the consideration of appointing a managing officer. General Townsend was already the chairman, Robert Macdonald was lead director, and the open position was president.

Townsend was a trim 64–year-old, with close-cropped hair and just over 6 feet tall. He opened the discussion with an observation: "This selection process is not like that found in business or other civilian organizations. It's more like a military process. We're looking to draft a volunteer for this position. With that, I'm turning the floor over to our lead director, Robert Macdonald."

"Thank you, general, all of you have received appropriate biographical data concerning our prospective volunteer. The format will be a back and forth question and answer session. I have, up to this point, only briefly discussed the position of president of our committee with the candidate. At this time I will introduce my nephew, Gordon Macdonald." There was a round of applause and then Robert MacDonald continued, "We'll take a short 15 minute break, then General Townsend will moderate the Q and A session."

Feigning a bit of indignation, Mac said to his uncle, "What makes you think I'm prepared or even want to go through this examination?"

"This will not be easy, but I think you have what it takes to be a good president. What do you think?" asked Uncle Bob.

"Maybe we'll find out in the next hour or so. I've told you before that I think this operation has a low chance of success. You may be surprised to hear that I have followed your adventures in this tax proposal. It is a brilliant idea for increasing wealth in America, however it is too large a disruption to the status quo for most people to embrace," said Mac.

"OK, my fellow committee members and I will see how you perform," said Uncle Bob.

Townsend resumed the session with a mission statement: "We have formed our Association to foster personal freedom and private property rights. Our government, as presently operating, is a threat! We aim to fix it!"

Attention shifted from the general to Mac with the expectation that Mac would respond to the mission statement.

Mac stood up and addressed the members: "There is not one person in this room who does not realize that all governments, including our own, depend upon force for their existence. Two of our greatest presidents and former generals – George Washington and Dwight D. Eisenhower - warned of excessive government power. Washington stated that government is force, a dangerous servant and a fearful master. Eisenhower identified and warned of the undue influence exerted by the government in concert with the military industrial complex. Even if you had no other point of reference, these warnings should be sufficient to seek to curb the excessive power of the IRS. It is true that any tax requires some sort of authority to collect. Not everyone will rush to the government with their tax payments on a purely voluntary basis.

"But it does seem to me that it should not be necessary for our government to be abusive to collect properly assessed taxes. As constituted, the income tax does seem to require abusive force to collect and therefore should be abolished.

"Let me ask about the committee's positions on other major tax issues that would favor one type of tax over another?" asked Mac.

Former Federal Reserve governor Martin Prescott responded: "From the perspective of coordinating monetary and fiscal policy in order to encourage economic growth and stability, the dollar yield from the income tax was often suspect in some way.

"On average it has failed to provide adequate funds for operating the government. Just look at the growing national debt for proof of that. It's lacking in flexibility in response to changing government requirements and its yield is not stable throughout business cycles. In short, it's not sufficiently adaptable.

"What is needed is a tax supported by a larger, more diversified base. I believe the consumption tax will fill that bill," concluded Prescott.

"Thank you for those observations, Governor Prescott," said Mac.

"Returning to the issue of force, it seems to me that if we aspire to reform government, we must also possess the ability to exert force," Prescott said. "Even non-military or non-police agencies in our government have a lot of guns. The IRS, for example, sports quite an arsenal."

"We cannot win a gun battle. I hope you have considered other forms of force," concluded Mac.

Townsend responded. "Our premise is that we can and must change the system, because it failed. The nation as a whole will do better and in particular, so will working class, or would be middle class Americans.

"You ask if we have considered force – we have. It comes in two forms: First we have a compelling plan which will correct the problem of stagnation which is afflicting our economy. Simply put, the U.S. has a national capital budgeting issue. Misallocation of resources has caused our society to become involved in a zero sum game. One person's gains must be another person's losses. It must not continue that way. Our plan will permit economic growth. Everyone willing to work can have a chance for prosperity.

"Our second element of force is money. We have a lot of it and we are focused on how to use it effectively. We have also considered the need for personal security and safety. We will not be sitting ducks," concluded Townsend.

The meeting went on with interchanges between Mac and the members and between members themselves.

Among other items, Adam Smith's four canons relating to proper taxation were discussed, including taxes should be levied according to one's ability to pay, be certain, not arbitrary, convenient to pay, and economical to collect.

Gordon Macdonald was offered and accepted the position as the Capital Club Association president.

As their flight returned to Santa Monica, Uncle Bob asked, "What do you think of the general?"

"I think he is a sharp guy. Do you know him well?" asked Mac.

"We have gotten to know each other over the past year or so. Among other things, I learned that we both served in Vietnam about the same time, 1968 to 1970, although under quite different circumstances. He was a pilot flying sorties into Cambodia to interdict North Vietnam and Viet Cong troops and supplies headed to South Vietnam. I was a sergeant stationed near Saigon, in the rear with the gear. Although I was not completely away from action. The Tet Offensive in 1968 almost got me. For a couple of days it was VC all over the place!" recalled Uncle Bob.

"Yeah, I know a bit about Vietnam. Knowing my dad died there made me want to understand what it was all about. The more I learned the less I think our country should have been there," replied Mac.

"In retrospect, many Americans think that way, including some who supported the war at the time," replied Uncle Bob

# Chapter 7

Jason West was an unlikely murderer at first glance. Physically unimposing, he was not a street thug, nor was he trained in martial arts or firearms. To the contrary, he was an accountant by trade and education. He was not a sad victim of a deprived childhood. As far as it could be observed, he got along with his parents, teachers and acquaintances while growing up. He had a privileged life; so where then did the ability to cause death originate?

As a college student, he was omnivorous. He envisioned a future as a power behind the throne, relatively obscure and thus difficult to identify as a target by his rivals and victims.

His choice of college reflected his under–the-radar approach. Cal-State Sacramento is a streetcar school with a middle tier reputation near the capitol of California. It was there that his concept of the throne that could be controlled and manipulated to his purposes was born. The government; what else?

Upon graduation he worked for the State of California Board of Equalization, the taxing arm of the state. Jason got the hang of using government power to his advantage. He soon realized it was small potatoes compared to the power play that could be had at the IRS.

Ten years into his tenure at the IRS, West, an upper mid-level bureaucrat, was running a shakedown operation hauling in millions of dollars. The mob could claim intellectual property theft.

Shakedown schemes require some sort of force to succeed and West's operation was no exception. He had at his disposal the vast authority vested in the IRS, for openers. As its size increased, the criminal enterprise became vulnerable to discovery and West knew it.

Like an addict, he couldn't shake the crime habit. Deadly violence was introduced when needed. Blackmail, bribery and other forms of cranial coercion will only get you so far. Eventually it becomes necessary to go violent.

Help along these lines was not far away. The Department of the Homeland Security (DHS), a relatively new group, has a record of bad behavior remarkable for even the government.

West went shopping for some muscle and discovered at the DHS James Barone, who did not come from a privileged background, and was trained in martial arts and firearms. His most recent gig was working for the private security force in Iraq, which was entrusted with the safety of civilian government officials, including diplomats. The security firm's tactics were a little rough, but they never lost a client. Actually they were very rough.

War makes strange bedfellows and it is the war on terror which gave cover to these two conspirators.

# Chapter 8

How in the world had things gone so wrong?

The United States of America began with high promise because it was founded by men who knew well the savage use of force by European governments. The very thing our representative republic had been designed to prevent has become its mode of operation: misuse of government power.

Mac's first day on the job was a mere five weeks and one day from the election. As he reflected on the task ahead, he realized the presidential part of the election would not be as important to our cause as the Legislature. Both major parties have put forth presidential candidates who are either unwilling to lead the way on a difficult issue or who are not up to speed on tax matters. What matters is the Congress. That is where the laws are made. There are 535 members to be contacted.

The Association's war room was military in style. The objectives were identified, assets available were identified, and the plan to win was mapped out.

The Association has no central headquarters because as Uncle Bob explained to Mac, "There is no question the federal government will identify and attempt to stop our activity. Our contact with 535 members of Congress is tantamount to going public. At the very least, we can expect the Internal Revenue Service, Department of Homeland Security, and the Federal Bureau of Investigation to take an interest in us. By the way, what's going on with Dugan?"

"Well, as you found out years ago, Dugan is a practical man. I met with him recently and we can retain his services which, although not explicitly specified, will include a significant amount of information regarding the IRS moves in our case," said Mac.

"As I'm sure you are aware, we have retained the services of South Bay Security. Would you ask Sarah to arrange for Dugan's employment with South Bay? He could be an independent contractor," said Uncle Bob.

"Yes, I will. Also, I would like to convene a meeting of the 28-member committee. What's your preference as to time and place?" asked Mac.

"In consultation with South Bay, the general and I have settled on a largely teleconference mode of meeting. Sarah has set up a secure network for us. For now, the war room is at the general's place in Carmel Valley. We can set up a meeting in a couple of days. You and I can fly in. You should have an agenda prepared ahead of time," said Uncle Bob.

The meeting was set for Wednesday. On the flight with Uncle Bob to Carmel Valley, Mac asked, "How secure is the general's place?"

"I don't know all the details except to say his military experience and high rank give him a head start. No government-instigated intrusion would commence without very high level sponsorship. We would expect a heads-up. Electronic and physical security is present and I assume up to the task," said Uncle Bob.

Townsend convened the meeting and greeted Robert and Gordon Macdonald.

"The objective we have is to influence Congress to vote to replace the federal income tax with other forms of taxation, principally a consumption levy. With that said, I will introduce our Executive Vice President William Walter, former governor of the state of Florida. The governor has joined us to head up our operational staff," said the general.

"Thank you, general. Let me discuss the politics and the economics of the tax reform we are proposing.

"Our opportunity rests with those Americans who don't manage tax-advantaged major corporations, labor unions or rely on welfare. That leaves most of Americans who are looking for a better tax system and upward income mobility. In fact, middle America is looking for a better system of government run by high-quality officials.

"One of the most sensitive issues when it comes to taxation and economic policy is that of fairness. You hear it when discussing income and wealth disparity of our citizens and the role government should play in correcting this problem. Many attempts have been made such as progressive income tax rates, minimum wage rates and a wide range of means tested government benefits. Yet those who seek even more government involvement in our economic affairs cite growing disparity of income and wealth as the reason to intensify the programs which have failed.

"In particular, since the income tax began, the U.S. has had progressive income tax rates, yet the distribution of income and wealth remains sharply tilted toward the upper groups, and the middle class and the lower income groups are becoming relatively worse off.

"What is going on here? Why hasn't the progressive taxation evened out income and wealth satisfactorily? Why hasn't our tax system been adequate to pay the government's expenses?

"I would start with Adam Smith's advice, which is to levy taxes in such a way as to cast a minimum burden upon the production of wealth. The tax system is best used as a way to raise funds to pay the government's expenses and not so much for regulatory purposes, sumptuary taxation or redistributing wealth. The latter three areas are where mischief occurs.

"The reason progressive tax rates have not seemed to result in meaningful redistribution of income, or wealth, is that there are other more powerful forces which determine the outcome. I think personal upward income mobility is the key. So long as individuals may pursue their own economic self-interest freely, within the rule of law, wealth will be distributed fairly, but not equally.

"The concept of tax neutrality has been developed and then cast aside. Three notions of tax neutrality deserve attention: First, 'leave them as you find them' permits people to retain their relative economic rank after taxation. Second, a neutral tax does not alter the allocation of resources. Third, a neutral tax assesses the tax burden independent of most choices made or actions taken by the taxpayer in regard to investments or methods of earning a living.

"The next point I will make on our tax system is that of concern for our civil liberties. The powers of enforcement bestowed upon the IRS for the collection of income taxes are beyond those ever fantasized about in most dictatorships. Combined with the tax laws for sale in Congress, you have the perfect playbook for the establishment of a self-perpetuating ruling class; that is, until the money runs out. Which brings me to my next point: The money has run out. The federal government is over-leveraged, unable to sustain its promises and unable to raise more revenue because each increase in tax rates decreases the tax base and therefore decreases tax revenue.

"With the more equitable and efficient method of taxation and the proper allocation of our resources, the U.S. will resume its historic pattern of rising standards of living," said the governor.

"How is the campaign going?" asked Mac.

"To begin with, we have a pretty good support program for candidates that agree; both financial and voter support. We have, or will obtain endorsements from government, labor, business and civic groups. If a congressperson will not support the program, our help will go elsewhere. The process of contact and soliciting support across party lines has been ongoing and now is at the point where we need a final push. The time period has been purposely compressed, because elements of our federal government, mainly the IRS and Justice Department, are likely to counterattack. Right now we have planned a major media event 10 days before the election. Our research shows that new candidates and ideas that catch on reach their zenith in one to two weeks. We will blitz the nation with press conferences by prominent people, TV, radio and newspaper ads and we'll use social media as well, to reach all types of people. We have booked media time and print space well in advance," said the governor.

"What we need now from all of you is to get a headcount of Congress members from your associates in the field – yes, no or maybe. Start with the leadership and work your way through the entire group," concluded Mac.

As Mac and Uncle Bob were preparing to depart, Townsend remarked, "Speaking of congressional support, I have heard of a significant reduction of effort and activity from the Tax Committee Chairman's Office lately. Although the killing of the senior congressional aide that was pushing for the consumption tax has not been connected to the tax issue so far, it does make me suspicious. There was talk of the incident being a hate crime because the individual was gay."

Uncle Bob was less circumspect, "What bullshit! I think the guy was whacked for his tax reform efforts!"

# Chapter 9

Alarms over the all-too-public Treasury funding debacle and declining tax revenues were spreading throughout the government. The thought that voter awareness of dangerous U.S. financial conditions would lead to a power shift away from the government was, well, unthinkable!

Massive data collection projects on U.S. citizens had become so large that they were useless. Garbage in, garbage out.

However, there were some bits of information culled from the sea of data that were pointing directly at a tax revolt. While it seemed to be spread over a diverse group of taxpayers, there was a growing effort to stop the income tax. Such an effort had to be nipped in the bud, or so thought some in government.

Inspector Jason West of the IRS convened a joint staff meeting with James Barone, his counterpart at the DHS. West presented his data on slowing tax collections, the emergence of large campaign contributions from previously obscure PACs, and antidotal evidence that there was an organized effort to influence Congress to deep-six the income tax.

At first, the reaction from the groups in attendance, other than the IRS, was laughter at the prospect of unemployment for the IRS agents. Then it began to sink in, that maybe none of these folks were all that secure if a power shift did occur.

A discussion ensued that boiled down to a few names of citizens that seemed to be involved. Newest of the government organizations involved in the discussion was the DHS. Its record of roughhouse, borderline criminal activity, covered up or justified by the Department of Justice, was spectacular. They were selected to be the shock troops. They were instructed to put an end to the tax strike and whatever other opposition they could find.

James Barone, the DHS representative, agreed. The role of enforcer fit Barone well. He had risen through the ranks of various private security firms and knew well the value of violence. He even looked the part, kind of like a retired linebacker. He was overweight, but at nearly 50 years old, he could still hold his own in a barroom brawl.


The second meeting of the Capital Club Association's committee under Mac's direction was held a week after the first. It was only four weeks to the election, and the nose count of Congress members was critical.

All 28 members of the Association's committee had reports. In the House of Representatives, more than 200 of the 435 members had indicated support for abolishing the federal income tax - one way or another. Another 50 were open to the idea. The Senate results were less positive, because only a third were up for election. It was natural that many would wait to see in what direction the wind was blowing. It was apparent that our heavyweight supporters from business and labor would need to be brought in for direct contact with the senators.

It was also reported by some associates that as the Association's efforts at reform became known, pushback from public employee unions, others in the government and certain outside groups, was increasing. Particularly dangerous are the IRS, the DHS, and it seems some private organizations.

Michael Lindberg, a 50-year-old attorney, had been selected and recruited as a regional associate because of his past and present relationships with both industrial employers and labor groups in Minnesota. Lindberg's duties included regional management of the PAC supporting the tax reform effort.

Behind the occasional headlines about the novelty type politicians elected in that state, there are a number of large, well-managed industrial and other business organizations. Relations between employers and employees, including those who were unionized, were generally constructive. It was fertile territory to generate support for the economic fix proposed by the Capital Club.

Lindberg's law firm was composed of two other partners; Cecilia Carlson, an attractive 45-year-old ash blond of medium height who had roots in Minneapolis; and Alan Jones, a 6-foot-5 former NFL Viking lineman who went to law school at Minnesota after his playing days were over and stayed put to practice law. A black man with a neatly trimmed beard and a full head of hair, and weighing in at 250 pounds, Alan Jones was an imposing figure.

Jason West, the IRS inspector, was on the phone to his counterpart at DHS, James Barone. "We've picked up some info that a lawyer from some two-bit law firm in Minneapolis is talking up the replacement of the income tax. Maybe you should send in a couple of your boys to see what it will take to shut this guy down. I can give you the names of two compliant federal judges who will issue a search warrant if you want one," said West.

"We'll just pay him a visit in his office without a search warrant – just to get an idea of what we're dealing with. I would like to have a local IRS agent come with us, because the subject of a possible tax audit is always intimidating," said Barone.

Agents Roberts and Wade from the DHS and agent Lucas from the IRS paid a visit to the Lindberg, Carlson & Jones Law Firm.

Michael Lindberg received the visitors; they struck Michael as an odd assortment. The two DHS men were both in their early 30s, about 6 feet tall, bulky, with short brown hair and seemed oversized for their suits. They looked like the muscle of the team.

Lucas, from the IRS, was older – probably in his late 40s, balding, a bit under 6 feet, carried an extra 20 or 30 pounds, and looked like the accounting type he was.

Lucas opened with, "We are concerned with the sudden appearance of PAC money directed to the attempt to replace the income tax. Who are the donors and where does the money come from?"

"You must be aware that information is provided in public filings that we've made, according to law?" said Lindberg.

"We are suspicious of its origin and legitimacy," said agent Wade.

"What's to be suspicious about?" asked Lindberg.

"We are paid to be suspicious," replied Wade.

"It's none of your business beyond what is contained in our public filings," said Lindberg.

"We think it is, and there will be additional issues from the IRS – think tax evasion, fraud – maybe even racketeer influenced and corrupt organization charges that should bring fear to those who might be accused of it. In fact, we know pretty much everything there is to know about you and we can come down on you like a ton of bricks. If you think it's just the IRS collecting your personal information, think again. We have data sharing arrangements with the Consumers Financial Protection Bureau who maintain, among other things, a national database containing your complete credit history and scores, not to mention performance data on credit cards and all types of loans. To make my point that we can really screw you, I'm going to read to you the following sentence from the Federal Register which states:"

*"'Where there is an indication of a violation or potential violation of law, whether civil, criminal or regulatory in nature, and whether arising by general statute or particular program statute, or by regulation, rule or order issued pursuant thereto, the relevant records in the system of records may be referred, as a routine use, to the appropriate agency, whether federal, state, local, tribal, foreign or a financial regulatory organization, including the Financial Crimes Enforcement Network and other law enforcement and government entities, as determined by FHFA to be appropriate and that are charged with the responsibility of investigating or prosecuting such violation or charged with*

*enforcing or implementing a statute, or rule, regulation or order issued pursuant thereto,'"* Wade finished with a smirk.

"You should consider the advantages of cooperating with us, since we are the government," said Lucas. "If you don't, you will be in a load of trouble. It won't be good for your reputation or your business. Think it over. Meanwhile, don't remove any records. We will be back with a search warrant later today."

"I'll stick around with you while Wade and Lucas get their warrant," said agent Roberts, who had not spoken up to then.

With Wade and Lucas on their way, Lindberg said to Roberts, "You should meet my two partners, I'll bring them in."

As Cecilia Carlson and Alan Jones entered, Lindberg made the introductions.

"This man and his associates, who happen to be on their way to get a search warrant for our office, think we are up to something illegal," said Lindberg.

"Such as?" asked Carlson.

"We think your activities are dangerous to the country and probably involve criminal activity," said Homeland Security agent Roberts.

"You don't say," remarked Carlson.

"This meeting is over," said Lindberg.

"I'm not leaving until my associates return with the search warrant," said agent Roberts.

"You're out of here!" said Cecilia Carlson, in her most professional, but forceful, tone.

Agent Roberts was surprised at Carlson's remark, but when Alan Jones rose with his 6-foot-5 frame and uttered his first word "goodbye," agent Roberts quickly departed.

Lindberg was on the line to Mac. "We have been rousted in our office by two muscle types from Homeland Security and an IRS agent who are making vague accusations and issuing threats to get a search warrant to search the office. They're gone for now, but what is our game plan?"

"Do you think they will return soon?" asked Mac.

"Yes," said Lindberg.

"I think you should call the local media to cover any removal of records or perp walk if they conduct one. We can portray this as one more bullying act by the Homeland Security thugs and the IRS. Meanwhile, one of our committee members, Maggie McFarland, a former federal judge, will get you some legal cover from your jurisdiction. We also have physical protection services available if you so request," said Mac.

Just before 5 p.m., the two Homeland Security agents accompanied by several U.S. marshals appeared with the promised search warrant. They usually call the media to embarrass the target of their raid, but this time the target arranged for the coverage. A prepared press release from the Lindberg, Carlson & Jones Law Firm was handed out to the reporters present. Basically it was a statement decrying government misdeeds, advocating replacement of the income tax and generally casting the government raiding party in a distasteful light.

The news coverage of the raid made the 11 p.m. national network news on the four broadcast organizations. Cable TV would follow the next day and evening.

"While it does appear that the government has suffered a p.r. setback, they have learned something of our organization and we must expect more pressure," said Mac on a conference call to the committee.

"We have contacted a number of federal judges in various districts who may be willing to deal with spurious requests for search warrants that will likely come from the DHS and IRS," said Maggie.

"Besides the DHS and IRS that will be largely dismantled under our plan, what other groups have expressed opposition to us?" asked Townsend.

"The 12,000 lobbyists in Washington D.C, are understandably dismayed at the prospect of no longer directing the dispensing of federal tax money, tax breaks and other favors to their clients," said Mac. "If we succeed in interrupting the flow of money in the money triangle, there will be significantly fewer lobbyists and legislators dependent on them. Public employee unions will fight our plan.

"Not surprisingly, there are some large corporate clients of the lobbyists who pay very little federal income taxes and so may not see a direct benefit in abolishing the income tax. Certainly their tax departments will not think it a good idea."

# Chapter 10

The election was only two days away.  The media campaign had run full out over the past two weeks, every congressperson was contacted and urged to publicly support the income tax repeal.  Polls on the subject were inconclusive.  Fierce opposition rose from certain groups as expected.

Before the election, Congress passed yet another continuing resolution to increase the national debt limit - enough to get by until the new administration took office the following January.  Of course inflation and interest rates were rising, but the main voter attention was focused on the presidential race, which included a progressive candidate from the party in power and a hard-to-define, all-over-the-map challenger from the other party.

The polls were not inconclusive on the presidential race: the challenger was getting creamed.  However, the polls were wrong and the challenger won the election.  At the same time, Congress was looking like it would trend a bit more conservative after the election.  Even so, it was apparent that the Capital Club's efforts at tax reform had failed at this point in time.  There are more voters than federal income taxpayers.

Mac convened a meeting of the 28-member committee.  They met at the general's ranch in Carmel Valley the day following the election.

Mac spoke first.  "It seems we got our ass kicked!  At one point we seemed to have the support of over 200 House members and 25 senators, but it was never more than a handshake type of commitment.  When the polls failed to confirm decisive public support for our proposition of doing away with the income tax, more than a few of our so-called supporters had second thoughts and faded away.  I'll now open the meeting to comments you may have."

Mark Nelson, the journalist member, said, "When you think about it, if we had gathered a supermajority support in Congress, it would have been astonishing - after all, we were asking congressmen who benefit as much as anyone to change the system that is rigged in their favor."

Martin Prescott, the former Federal Reserve official, commented, "It's really hurtful to the country to face an inevitable long-term diminution of the standard of living. The only way to counteract the inevitable rise in interest rates and the crushing burden that will place on the economy generally, and the cost of government debt specifically, is to allow inflation to rise, thus creating cheaper dollars. Inflation is the hidden tax that will allow the Treasury to continue for some time to pay its obligations by borrowing even more. Of course the money markets will demand higher rates and probably shorter terms, because they know repayment will be made with cheap dollars."

John Reed, the banker, said, "I think the system will eventually grind to a near collapse. Widespread economic deprivation does not make for happy citizens. If our newly elected president pans out like the predecessor, we will be enduring the third straight failed presidency – 16 years and counting!"

Lunch was served and the topic changed to what the Capital Club Association members might expect in retaliation from the various government, business and union opponents.

Maggie McFarland said, "I have retained a number of law firms around the country on a standby basis to deal with any legal type harassment we may receive. In addition, Sarah, from South Bay Security, has developed a program for electronic and if necessary, physical protection. We also have a source for some information about possible IRS moves they may undertake.

"Most dangerous besides the IRS, is the Department of Homeland Security. It is the newest department, now larger than the Department of Justice, and by the government's own figures, significantly prone to committing crimes.  It is a collection of some well-established and managed elements such as the Coast Guard, Secret Service, Customs and Border Patrol.  Other elements are new or expansions of some of the above and appear poorly managed."

Uncle Bob, who has taken the debacle hard, came to life. "I can't believe our cause is finished!" he said. "The system can't survive as is!  Many voters are pacified now, but as the economy tanks, that will change.  We need to hang in there so when the opportunity opens up, we can take another shot.  I'll ask Mac and the general to join me in formulating a kind of hibernation plan, keeping our resources intact while we decide our future.  I hope all or most of you stay on board."

# Chapter 11

Jason West of the IRS and James Barone of the DHS met following the election. They were in a somewhat celebratory mood as their congressional allies had won the election.

West, by far the more senior in authority and superior in financial skills of the two, had stepped up his game of getting rich earlier in his government service. Many in government service monetize their influence after they depart the government, but not Inspector West – he had conceived of, developed and managed the secret and entirely illegal Supplementary Pension Fund for the benefit of certain government agents who could extort or cause to be made significant monetary contributions in return for regulatory favors. Its existence and success depended on under-the-table administration at the IRS - thanks to West. The fund had grown quite large over the years. It is based on the same idea that a local building inspector uses to ignore a code violation or to expedite a permit in exchange for a bribe. The difference here is that the U.S. Congress is the foil. Poorly or vaguely written legislation leaves a lot of room for interpretation, which can enhance or kill economic opportunity in the private sector.

A portion of the funds collected goes to what could be described as the beat cops. But the larger portion goes to the Supplementary Pension Fund , which goes offshore.

As they retire, a lump sum is made available offshore to each of the participants; no wonder they choose to live outside the U.S. After all, the U.S. Treasury will send their well-earned regular government pension checks to any location. Those are not the checks that support the mansions, yachts and other perks of the rich – if not the famous.

Inspector West does not really care about what kind of tax system we have; what he does care about is the ability to use the system to extort money.

Sounding a note of caution despite their election victory, West remarked, "As long as we keep winning elections, we will probably be OK. As far as our phony audits are concerned, cover-up is what we do best. There was one time a few months ago, before the election, that I heard some rumors about the possibility of some negative information leaking out. It's a good thing that matter was taken care of. Otherwise the opposition might have come across what we really do. We are talking about control of the government here and all the goodies that go with it. Someone high up evidently took action."

Barone, more of a street enforcer type, thought for a moment and then said, "Now that you mention it, that was about the time your commissioner was killed in a hit-and-run incident."

"Barton was just an outsider who had no place here. Good riddance," said West.


Following the election, Ed Dugan maintained his contacts with his former colleagues at the IRS. It was thus that he had picked up some chatter about a campaign to clamp down on those citizens known to have actively opposed the income tax.

Both Robert and Gordon Macdonald were on the IRS radar screen. Mindful of almost certain IRS surveillance of political targets, Ed chose Sarah at South Bay Security, their common employer, as his communication go-between with Mac.

At first, the IRS contacts had the trappings of ordinary audits. As the audits dragged on like a bad cold, Uncle Bob began to realize it was the source of the PAC funding that the IRS was after. It appeared that Ed Dugan's earlier heads-up was spot on.

Just after the holidays, Mac, Sarah, Maggie and Uncle Bob gathered at Uncle Bob's place for an NFL playoff game. Uncle Bob and Maggie seemed to have rekindled their relationship.

As the football game wound down, the subject of the IRS was visited.

"I'm concerned about the extent the IRS is going to in this audit process," said Uncle Bob.

"I am too," said Mac. "What has Dugan reported lately?"

"Dugan reports that there's a lot more to the opposition to our tax reform efforts than you might expect considering our campaign was shot down in flames!

"Several of our committee members and associates in various parts of the country have experienced SWAT-type raids," said Maggie. "They have been conducted by various regulatory agencies with the support of the DHS. It seems like mission creep to have non-police agencies, such as regulatory organizations, conducting armed raids for alleged white collar or civil offenses."

"That's not comforting," said Uncle Bob. "Maybe it's time for a vacation trip somewhere private."

"I may be able to help with that," said Sarah. "Our firm has some interesting associates who are able to provide off-the-record travel and housing if needed."

"To start with, I think staying out of sight in Southern California would be best to start with. If need be, I could reappear quickly and easily. My lawyer and accountant already are involved with the audit," said Uncle Bob.

Sarah arranged for a two-week cruise along the California coast on a private 45-foot catamaran with crew. Uncle Bob was more than satisfied with that and invited Maggie to go along. Their relationship, rekindled over the recent political campaign, was a much-needed spark in their lives.


James Barone had become impatient. The IRS audit of Robert Macdonald was going nowhere. It was time to intimidate him. The only problem was that Macdonald was nowhere to be found. Telephone and credit card surveillance revealed nothing. A stakeout of Macdonald's home came up empty. It was time to get agents Roberts and Wade back into action.

Barone set the plan in motion. Roberts and Wade would shift over to Gordon Macdonald to start with. The office visit would come on Friday at 5 p.m. straight up.

Mac's office is small, containing two rooms and a reception area shared with dozens of other small businesses. Most of the people working in the building were in the process of leaving or had already left for the day when agents Roberts and Wade strode in.

The agents flashed their DHS IDs and confronted Mac, who was seated at his desk.

"This is an administrative search to enforce regulatory law," said agent Roberts as he presented a search warrant and a list of documents. "You are suspected of various financial crimes and as a result, you are required to surrender records pertaining to the following items."

"You boys get right to the point - no small talk," said Mac, and then added, "This is nothing but bullying!"

Roberts, who had been reading from a script, went ad lib: "You think this is bullying? If I had my way, you'd be face down right now! They tell me to play nice because you are some sort of privileged asshole who shouldn't be touched. Don't push it or you'll find out different."

"You might find out something different yourself," replied Mac.

"We have additional agents on their way in, who will remove your records to our custody. If you resist in any way, you will be restrained and possibly arrested," said agent Roberts.

When the agents completed their collection process, Mac made a private call to Sarah on their secure line.

"Sarah, the DHS just entered my office and grabbed my computer

and other records and files.  They may pay a visit to our house, too.
I'm sure they have some surveillance in place, so there is not much we
can do at the moment.  Call Maggie's law firm and bring them up to
date.  I'll see you at home around seven," said Mac.

"Good grief!  We send Uncle Bob away on a trip and the DHS lands
on us!," she said. "I think we should keep me in the background as
much as possible.  No need to steer them to me or South Bay Security.
I'll have one of our field operators keep an eye on the condo.  South
Bay can make a reservation and pay for a room at the Biltmore in Santa
Barbara.  I'll pick you up at the Yacht Club and we'll be gone for the
weekend."

"As usual, you have the best plan.  See you around seven at the
Club," said Mac.

The weekend was a time of reflection.

"Aggressive contact from the government will force a change in our
operation.  Agent Roberts said he would like to put me face down," said
Mac.

"We are not the only people under duress from our government,"
replied Sarah. "In fact, to serve its clients, who are quite diverse, South
Bay has safe houses, means of transport that are quite private and an
affiliated agency out of the U.S."

"The raid has netted nothing of value to the DHS, just as the ongoing IRS audit has come up empty," Mac said. "Records relating to
financial matters of the Capital Club are in deep storage and have been
for some time."

"I'm worried that the IRS and the DHS agents will become more
aggressive in this matter," said Sarah.

"Maybe they are on the way," replied Mac.  And indeed they were
- surveillance had been set up at Robert Macdonald's residence by the
feds.

Uncle Bob and Maggie had returned late evening from their cruise off the California coast. After dropping off Maggie at her house, Uncle Bob proceeded to his own home and went to bed. He was awakened from a sound sleep at the break of dawn by the clanging of his burglar alarm and the violent sound of a door being broken down. Uncle Bob grabbed his bedside revolver and confronted the intruders.

Mac received the call at 10 a.m. that day in his office.

Uncle Bob had been shot and killed in an early morning "knock and announce" raid at his home by armed federal agents, including U.S. marshals.

The caller was from the LAPD, who arrived on the scene in response to a 911 call from a neighbor. Details were scant, but they referred to the raid as an enforcement action to obtain evidence in a suspected financial crime.

For the moment, Mac was immobilized. How could it be that Uncle Bob was shot by feds who were looking for files? Upon regaining his bearings, Mac called Sarah.

"Sarah, Uncle Bob is gone," said Mac.

"What are you talking about?" asked Sarah anxiously.

"He was shot dead in a confrontation with the feds at home. I don't know much more at this point."

"Oh, my God! What about Maggie? Does she know about it yet?" asked Sarah.

"For all we know, she may be on the investigator's list too. I think we should both go see her and let her know," said Mac.

They met at Maggie's house and Mac broke the news to Maggie. Maggie was stunned with grief and Sarah attempted to comfort her. As Mac observed that interaction, his own feelings of loss and rage began to intrude on his consciousness.

The process of dealing with the shooting death of Uncle Bob began in the usual ways: First an autopsy by the county, then the funeral, followed by confirmation of Mac as the administrator of Robert

Macdonald's estate. Mac got lawyered up and began the process of confronting the various government agencies involved.

It was only the fact that Uncle Bob was well known, in a positive way, by the West LAPD brass, that the crime scene at Uncle Bob's home had not been scrubbed by the feds.

Officers initially responding to the 911 call quickly relayed Uncle Bob's identity and condition to the watch commander. The LAPD aggressively took control of the scene, interviewed witnesses and found, among other things, that Uncle Bob's pistol had not been fired. Mac learned, off the record, that along with the gun issue, the front door was broken down for no apparent reason, other than to frighten and intimidate Uncle Bob. Because of the violent methods used to enter, this raid amounted to a no-knock operation, which was outlawed decades earlier. A real knock and announce raid must give the target time and opportunity to respond to the announcement.

News of the killing spread quickly through the committee and in the Los Angeles business and social community. The feds were stonewalling and inferring an unspecified criminal behavior on Robert Macdonald's part.

Because of Uncle Bob's strong standing in the community, including a successful business and generous philanthropy, there was public pushback.

The public outcry was reaching higher levels in the government than those who instigated and carried out the raid that killed Uncle Bob. Would that matter?

## Chapter 12

General Townsend, the chairman, called a meeting of the committee shortly following the election. The general had an ambitious agenda to chart a new course for the Capital Club.

Liberal or conservative, most elected officials saw that divided government power gave them leverage over the private sector. With political contributions from favor-seeking business and labor unions and expanding welfare programs to govern the poor, all the bases were covered.

"I have convened this meeting of the committee in order to select two new officers: First we need a lead director to replace Robert Macdonald, who as you know, was killed in a forced entry raid in his home by a rogue DHS agent, or so we've been told. Secondly, we need to select a new president to replace his nephew, Gordon Macdonald, who has resigned to attend to personal matters.

"Our member, John Reed, has agreed to serve as lead director and I ask that you confirm that appointment. Hearing no objections, I declare that motion approved.

"As you all have been informed, our executive vice president, Governor William Walter, has been asked to replace Gordon Macdonald as our president. I'll now turn the floor over to Governor Walter, who will convey his take on America's opportunities and what we should do about them," said Townsend.

"In my experience as governor of a non-income tax state, I have learned that winning political support and elections depends on gaining influence on several important issues which necessarily involve diverse groups. I believe this was our downfall in the first attempt to get rid of the income tax. It was presented as a single issue. Not a sufficient number of power groups perceived the changed tax system that we proposed would be in their interest. In fact more than a few in large corporations and other enterprises have gamed the tax system to the extent that they think everything is OK at their headquarters. Labor unions buy their political favors and recipients of federal payments of one sort or another, fear change.

"Would the change from federal income taxes to consumption taxes begin to solve America's financial and social problems? Would it change in a positive way, the relationship between the individual and the state? In a word, yes. Can we get it done? Apparently not."

Walter continued. "What can we do? I think there are a few things. One is to join with advocates of reforming the tax code and selectively cutting income tax rates. On the other side of the ledger is the need to restrain government spending.

"From a civil liberties perspective, we must form a watchdog group to expose the corruption at the IRS and other deep state operations. How much worse does criminal behavior need to be, before something is done?" concluded the governor.

Townsend returned to the podium. "Thank you, governor, for those remarks. I'm now calling upon those assembled here to approve your appointment as our president and manager. Hearing no objection, I declare that motion approved."

# Chapter 13

The Department of Homeland Security and James Barone in particular were feeling the heat over the killing of Robert Macdonald. The usual veil of protection from the Attorney General's Office at the Department of Justice was showing cracks.

At first the Department of Homeland Security issued the standard "we are investigating and if anyone did anything wrong they will be held accountable" statement. Then came the slow walk of the investigation, which is designed to take a long time in hopes that the public will forget.

The Department of Justice, however, was not so insulated from the public outcry over Robert Macdonald's shooting. The LAPD crime scene report was becoming more widely circulated and it did not flatter the DHS raiders. Calls for an actual investigation by the FBI were coming from many quarters, some quite influential.

Barone was becoming apprehensive because instead of being asked about the raid and how to justify it, he was being ignored. But not for long.

The meeting was called by an upper level lawyer at the Department of Justice. The invitee was the assistant secretary of Homeland Security and the subject of this meeting was the killing of Robert Macdonald.

"It seems we have, or maybe just you have, a real cluster fuck on your hands," said the lawyer.

"We're working on it," said the assistant secretary. "Our investigation will take a while. Maybe the furor will subside over time and we can create some story that will discredit the victim."

"Have you read the LAPD crime scene report?" asked the lawyer. "Do you know the history of the victim? Well regarded in the community, he will not be easily smeared. What the hell is the matter with you clowns?"

Taken aback by the use of the term victim in reference to Macdonald, the assistant secretary was beginning to realize someone nearby was going to take the fall.

"What do you want me to do?" asked the assistant secretary.

"Who is this guy Barone?" asked the lawyer.

"He's a supervising field agent with a lot of experience in politically and legally sensitive missions. In fact, he used to work for you folks in the Department of Justice. I think he was a border agent back then. When necessary or expedient, he uses contract personnel," answered the assistant secretary.

"What I want you to do is spin the customary rogue agent story, quietly get rid of Barone and any contract personnel he used on this caper, and make it possible for them to disappear. Settle their finances and legal status so they have no incentive to speak about any of this," the lawyer said. "If there is legal action to come from the victim's family, we will settle at our end. I want Barone out of the picture."

Early in the discovery period following Uncle Bob's death, Mac retained an attorney recommended by Maggie. Ronald Steel knew his way around the government, having been a prosecutor as well as a defense attorney.

Steel's assignment was to sift through the evidence including LAPD reports and Department of Homeland Security statements to help determine the why and who of the crime. It was clear that the process would take some time. The big stall was on.

During the past 10 years of Ronald Steel's 30-year career in law, he had become involved on the victim's side of a number of so-called tactical entry cases where doors were kicked down, homes and offices raided, and citizens taken into custody. All too often, the issues pursued by the various government agencies were financial, administrative or political in nature; not violent crime where gun-toting, door-smashing police might be expected.

Steel, with a friendly demeanor, was not intimidating when first met. Average height with a full head of gray hair, medium build and well dressed, it wasn't until well into a witness deposition or trial examination that his high skill and tenacity became fully appreciated.

He was socially acquainted with Robert Macdonald in a minor way, along with some other members of the Association's committee. Steel was aware of the anti-income tax effort under way, but had no reason to connect it with Robert Macdonald's killing. That perception would change after meeting with Mac several weeks following Uncle Bob's death.

Mac broached the subject. "Your report on the DHS response to our inquiry into the killing was revealing in that the DHS says it was an accident. They didn't say specifically why they were there in the first place."

"That's right," replied Steel.

"Did you get any indication of why it was a night raid?" asked Mac.

"No. It's clear they don't want to create much of a public record, because they know how wrong this was and how bad it will reflect on the department. In particular, they don't want the reason for the raid to come out," said Steel.

"I know what the reason was," said Mac.

"What was it and how do you know?" asked Steel.

"During the campaign, various associates were raided and otherwise harassed by the IRS and DHS agents. Those actions mostly ceased after the election, but I think they are worried about the future and in this case intended to eliminate a higher up leader of the movement, my uncle, and it went just as planned," said Mac.

"If you are correct, they will want to settle quietly off the record.

What do you want me to go for?" asked Steel.

"I've thought about it a lot. Make a push for some kind of financial settlement for show, but what I really want are the names of those involved. I want to know who pulled the strings and who pulled the trigger," said Mac.

"I can understand your anger and desire to put a face to the crime, but I think they'll strongly resist revealing that information," said Steel.

"Why can't we file a lawsuit in the U.S. Court of Federal Claims which will give us an opportunity for discovery? There are public and internal reports of the event from both the LAPD and the DHS. We can get depositions from the key players. Let's find out what the DHS and IRS have to say. I want those boys prosecuted and put away," said Mac.

# Chapter 14

Sarah knew in her heart what Mac would do about Uncle Bob's murder. He would extract revenge. She chose a quiet Saturday morning to speak to Mac about it.

"Mac, it's been a month since Uncle Bob was taken from us and I can understand that you're somewhat morose and preoccupied about it – but you seem to be slipping to the dark side! I'm worried about you and quite frankly, I'm worried about us too! Talk to me babe," she pleaded.

"I don't feel much like talking about it right now," said Mac as he turned away from her.

"Of course you don't! That's the macho way and I'm not buying it!" taunted Sarah.

"Call it what you want, but that's the way it is," replied Mac.

"Well, I don't know about you, but I'm going to kick some ass! Someone in the government, or working for the government, has murdered a law-abiding U.S. citizen who also happened to be our Uncle Bob! Notice I said our Uncle Bob? So, are you going to help me or not?" yelled Sarah.

For the first time in recent weeks, Mac allowed himself to relax and smile over Sarah's outburst. "It looks like I'd better get involved. My first choice is to push the government to prosecute, convict and jail whoever did this murder. There is likely to be a chain of individuals responsible and they will make every effort to cover it up. Failing that, you should know that I think the nature of the crime committed calls for an extra legal response," said Mac.

"By that, do you mean you're going to kill someone or cause

someone to die?" asked Sarah.

"Probably, but I don't want you involved. Uncle Bob was my family," said Mac.

Sarah was fighting to hold back tears. "Don't try to leave me out of the family. I want in because I can help you. Aren't we family? You and I?"

They fell into an embrace and the deal was sealed.

"It will mean quite a change in our life," said Mac. "I don't see this as an assault on the government as an entity. It makes no difference to me where they work. They could be gang members or unemployed. They killed Uncle Bob – that's all that matters to me. It's strictly personal. Some part of the DHS will be on the hunt for years – maybe our whole lives," said Mac.

"OK, just so I understand, there are three parts to this: first, we ID the bad guys; second, if the government fails to act, we do the killing; and third, we stay out of the government's grasp?" asked Sarah.

"If we both embark on this mission, the third part should be in place before the first and second. I can't believe you are willing to do this," said Mac.

"It's time for a road trip," said Sarah.

"Thinking about getting a safe house," said Mac.

"We'll need one at some point," replied Sarah.

"Along those lines, I have set up some entities for other purposes that will be helpful here," said Mac. "There exist two organizations with international operations that I control through trusts and partnerships including a small bank in the South Pacific which are not traceable directly to me. They are for the purpose of moving money around without attracting attention."

"In the past, you mentioned a wine importer from New Zealand that you had an interest in. Is that one of them?" asked Sarah.

"Yes, it is. It's named Cask and operates with a New Zealand attorney who serves as manager at present. The other is Vacation Partners based in Nevada. Its business offices are managed by an attorney in Reno. Among other things, it has an SUV with Nevada plates that we can use," said Mac.

The road trip actually began in the air, on a private charter from Santa Monica, California to Reno, Nevada. Upon landing in Reno, they went to the year-old GMC SUV and prepared to drive for parts as yet unknown.

"Before we move on from the Reno area, I think we should tie down something here – don't you? It's easy to get to, lots of people coming and going, and we can remain pretty much unnoticed," said Mac.

Vacation Partners had leased a three-bedroom condo in a vacation rental type place just outside of town, and then they set off to find the second place.

As they drove through northern Nevada, eastern Oregon and southern Idaho, there was ample time to contemplate their plan.

"If you think about who has been successful at defying the rule of law, it has been criminal and business enterprises with enough resources to corrupt the government and in particular politicians and law enforcement. Then as a result, it is the government itself which defies the law," said Sarah.

"We have found that out the hard way. Corruption in the IRS is pervasive and so far no one is being prosecuted. I think a little self-help is needed here," replied Mac.

"How do you see that working?" asked Sarah.

"I don't know exactly. We already have Ed Dugan, who can help with the IRS. Maybe we'll get someone like that with the DHS who can finger the person who is leaning on the income tax abolitionists - all we need is an ID. I don't care if it takes a year or two to finish, as long as the job gets done," said Mac.

A week into the road trip, they made their way to Coeur d'Alene in northern Idaho. They decided it would be the next place, after Reno, that would work for the 'disappear in plain sight' plan.

"I remember this town from years ago, when I passed through on a hunting trip," said Mac.

"Speaking of hunting, my brother, Cliff, is a hunting guide and out-fitter just north of here in Montana," said Sarah.

"I remember Cliff, we met a couple years ago. He had just finished a four-year hitch with the Marine Corps. Have you been in contact lately?" asked Mac.

"We talk occasionally, but Cliff isn't all that social," said Sarah.

"When I asked him about his experiences in the Iraq War, he said he was with a recon squad. Then I asked how he kept alive, he said they worked at night," said Mac.

"That sounds like Cliff. Short answers, to the point," said Sarah.

## Chapter 15

Ed Dugan was proving his worth. Within the past six months, as the negotiations with Steel and the Department of Justice lawyers were dragging along, Dugan had found a kind of informal whistleblower in the DHS.

For a mid-five-figure dollar amount, Dugan's informant gave up the names of three DHS personnel who seemed to fit the description of those who pulled the strings and pulled the trigger.

Sarah received Dugan's report from South Bay Security. As she and Mac read the single page, they learned only half of what they needed. All three had left the service and had conveniently disappeared.

"I know two of these guys – agents Roberts and Wade from the DHS," said Mac.

"How do you know them?" asked Sarah.

"They came to my office on one of their administrative raids," said Mac.

"How about the other guy?" asked Sarah.

"Never heard of Barone," said Mac. "Seems he was an older mid-level DHS agent. They probably gave him early retirement. The other two might still be working somewhere. They are in their early 30s, too young to actually retire."

"The affiliated agency out of the country I spoke of is named Investors Services and is located in Vancouver, British Columbia. It has resources including private investigations such as skip tracing on a high level. They are able to work on a very confidential basis. If you are ready to get started, I can set up a search assignment. I think they can help," said Sarah.

"What is their background and what kind of work have they done?" asked Mac.

"South Bay originally hooked up with Investors Services in connection with some international money laundering. South Bay's client was a financial institution that was victimized by an Islamic group, mainly from Pakistan, in their activities of financing propaganda and possibly terrorist efforts in the U.S.," said Sarah.

"Investors Services sounds kind of benign. Hardly what you would expect for some rough work," said Mac.

"Don't be fooled. The firm is run by R.J. Singh, who is a native of India and has been active in the conflict with radical Muslims for quite some time," said Sarah.

"How does that fit with our problem? We're not in conflict with any Muslims that I'm aware of," said Mac.

"No, but maybe the two younger ex-DHS agents are. The demand for private security comes not only for protection against common crime, but to a greater extent from organizations operating where Islamic pirates, terrorists or rebels threaten personnel and property," said Sarah.

"I see your point. They were eased out of DHS to minimize the effectiveness of our quest for information about the raid on Uncle Bob's house. Then they could be expected to migrate to private security requiring the same skill set," said Mac.

"That's why Singh's outfit, Investor Services, might be the best source to find Roberts and Wade," said Sarah.

"How do you see us engaging their services? What do we tell them about why we want to find those two? After all, it's not too tough to figure out that if someone you have been hired to locate winds up dead after you found him, the person who hired you might have something to do with the killing," said Mac.

"Do you think, maybe?" said Sarah.

"Let's put the search assignment to Singh through a small law firm and see what turns up. We'll be the law firm's unnamed client," said Mac.

"Do you have one in mind?" asked Sarah.

"Maybe our lawyer who looks after our New Zealand wine firm would suit the job," said Mac.

"Tell me about this lawyer and your wine operation," said Sarah.

"Several years back I requested Robert Chancellor of the Parnell Law Firm in Auckland to establish a wine export organization centered in the Hawkes Bay area. So far there are half a dozen wineries supplying Cask with wines for export. The purpose was to provide a business reason for transactions and travel between New Zealand and the U.S. Now we can add Vancouver and the rest of British Columbia to the list.

"I have a non-exclusive wholesale distributer to sell on the West Coast. There is enough activity in the business to bury from sight our search effort," said Mac.

"I know R.J. personally. I can pave the way for Chancellor to engage Investors Services. The arrangement will not reveal our involvement," said Sarah.

"Do it," said Mac.


Three weeks into the search, Investors Services came up with information on Roberts and Wade including the fact that Mac and Sarah are not the only ones interested.

"I'm sure you recall the death of the IRS commissioner, Anderson Barton, about a year ago. It was reported as a hit-and-run accident. But his wife, Mary, does not buy that story and has retained private investigators that R.J. cooperates and works with. It turns out that Barton was a high-powered guy in D.C. politics before the IRS and as a result Mary has a fair amount of residual influence. Basically, it comes down to Barton for some reason was going to bust the IRS criminal activities and he was killed for his efforts. It may have been Roberts and Wade who killed him," said Sarah.

"Lay it on me. Where are those two pricks?" asked Mac.

"They both have been in Nigeria with one of the security firms that have followed in the footsteps of private security organizations in Iraq and Afghanistan. As you may recall, their method attracted some bad press, but on the other hand, it is reported that they never lost a client.

"Roberts seems to have fallen out of favor for erratic behavior. He is being let go and our source tells us he is headed back home to Montana. I presume we'll be able to track him down, but then what? He is a very dangerous opponent," said Sarah.

"True, but at least he is no longer a U.S. government employee. I think he is now a much easier target. Let's put a tail on him and find out what he does and where he lives," said Mac.

The surveillance report came to Sarah just over a month after Roberts landed in Libby, Montana.

"We have some good stuff on our friend Roberts, but nothing yet on Wade. It seems Roberts is living in a doublewide mobile home adjacent to town. He doesn't spend too much time there because his old friends are mostly gone from the area. It seems he has hooked up with a survivalist group around Clark Fork, in northern Idaho. He drinks too much and goes off on rants about his bad treatment in life," said Sarah.

"He sounds like an accident waiting to happen! Go ahead and call off the surveillance. It's only about 70 miles from here to his place in Montana. We can take it over ourselves.

"Since we already located Roberts, let's ask Steel to get his deposition. If he fails to respond, I think we can get U.S. Marshals to serve an order to comply. He will probably lawyer up and stall or take the fifth. What we can accomplish is to let him know we are on his tail. If he becomes aggressive, we can deal with that. On the other hand, he may want to cut a deal before this case becomes a criminal matter. At this point our case is asking for damages and the DHS has not admitted that a crime was committed. Whether or not to prosecute for the killing has not been decided.

The idea of moving on to Reno seemed like a good thing to Mac and Sarah.

"I've been watching the local news for anything about Roberts over the past week since he was served with his deposition notice," said Sarah. "The only thing I saw is a missing person report filed by his girlfriend, two days after his disappearance. The story she told was pretty limited in scope – she knows after a night of drinking at the Bridge Saloon, that Roberts isn't around any longer and that's about it. It's pretty clear he's gone on the lam."

They made it a two-day trip from Coeur d'Alene to Reno. As they approached their destination, Mac received a call from Ronald Steel regarding Steel's investigation.

"I have some interesting late-breaking news," said Steel.

"It's been on my mind to review with you our case with the Department of Justice – what have you got?" asked Mac.

"I've heard from James Barone. As you know, the DHS showed him the door a year or so ago. They went cheap on the severance package and now Barone wants to be a whistleblower. He figures we have a case and he can put the finishing touches to it. It would be a nice settlement for us and him to share. So he thinks," said Steel.

"Incredible! I'm more than surprised! I'd like to get back with you on this tomorrow if that works for you. We've been driving quite a long time today and need to settle in for the night," said Mac.

"OK, tomorrow at 10 a.m. I'll be in my office and have a secure line for us," said Steel.

"Turning to Sarah, Mac spoke, "Good grief! What do you make of that?"

"It sounds like Barone was just a mid-level bureaucrat who thought he was a team player. Maybe he didn't know the level of violence his shock troops were committing. In any event, he is not playing on the DHS team anymore," said Sarah.

"Let's find out what Steel counsels first. My guess is we may meet with Barone," said Mac.

Promptly at 10 a.m., Steel answered Mac's call. "Since we spoke yesterday, I have learned that Barone is living in Florida and has lawyered up. This makes a lot of sense for him, because not only are we looking to pin a crime on him, so too will his former employer."

"Do you think we should attempt to get a statement from him?" asked Mac.

"Initially, we need to find out what kind of an arrangement he wants and generally what he has to offer. For sure he will want whistleblower status. Let me meet with his lawyer before we try to talk with Barone personally," said Steel.

"Alright, what else is going on?" asked Mac.

"I think we're making some progress. They would like to make it go away before it becomes even more public. The Department of Justice is talking a seven figure settlement with you. The first number is one at the moment. I'll report back to you on my conversation with Barone's lawyer," said Steel.

Barone was in a pensive mood. A 25-year career, which could have been 30 years, cut short by the actions of overly aggressive enforcer types. "Roberts and Wade screwed up and I get the door," he brooded. "Where is the loyalty? The top brass wants the political opposition pushed around – I do it for them and then I'm off the team and they shorted me on my severance package to boot! Of course I'm going to get even!"

The sun was setting into the Gulf of Mexico and Barone was half in the bag sitting on his balcony. He barely felt the prick of the needle in his arm. Then more distinctly, he felt himself propelled back into his apartment where he was about to die from an apparent drug overdose.

The maintenance man quickly set the stage for an obvious drug overdose and left the way he had entered, through the front door with a pass key. Once in his service truck driving away from the scene, Wade thought back on his time working for Barone.

"Here was that big fat-ass senior clerk giving me orders and then running away when the going got tough. Working off the books for the government was much preferred to his former official position. Besides a much better pay scale, he wasn't even required to pay income taxes on it. Who wouldn't go for that? One down and two to go," Wade thought.

# Chapter 17

When the Capital Club threw in with the new administration on its version of tax reduction and reform, it placed the campaign for elimination of the federal income tax in an induced coma.

The economic heavyweights have spoken. The big money movers and shakers knew the economy needed a shot in the arm and they had a very good idea on how to do it. Cut corporate tax rates almost in half and provide for a nearly meaningless shuffle of individual tax rates and income brackets.

Remarkably, the tax measure passed through Congress and was signed into law by the president.

Initial reaction was positive with corporations announcing all sorts of plans for salary increases, share buybacks and capital investments. Capital from offshore havens returned. The economy and stock market improved and most Americans felt better off.

It was a bittersweet development for Mac and Sarah. The corrupt IRS was still in business. The positive part is the notion that capital will flow to the highest after tax risk adjusted return was validated. The U.S. economy was booming.

The new tax plan was good for the IRS. Thousands of pages of new regulations provide nearly limitless opportunities for mischief. For inspector James West, it was not all good news. His former comrade in arms, the recently cashiered James Barone, had been found dead of a drug overdose. On top of that, Mrs. Barton, the wife of the deceased IRS commissioner, had publicly stated her husband's death was an inside job and she could prove it.

New investigations and threatened lawsuits were increasing the pressure on West and his hidden Supplementary Pension Fund. The silver lining, or perhaps the golden lining, was the $220 million of undisbursed funds remaining in the plan.

# Chapter 18

Steel's follow-up report was a complete surprise. "There won't be any meeting with Barone. He's dead; an apparent drug overdose."

Mac was stunned momentarily and then said, "This doesn't look right to me. Do you think it had anything to do with Barone's intention to turn on his former employer?"

"I don't know. Maybe he had an addictive personality that kicked in under stress. Or maybe he was murdered," said Steel.

"I appreciate how quickly you were able to learn the news and relay it to me. Go ahead with the government settlement discussions as if nothing has changed. See if there is any difference in attitude at their end," said Mac.

"OK, Mac, I'll let you know as soon as possible," said Steel as he hung up.

"You say Barone was found dead of a drug overdose?" exclaimed Sarah. "Right in the midst of making arrangements to rat out the Department of Homeland Security and you don't know if he was murdered or not?"

"Well, I ..."

"Hold up a minute, they had him killed – I know they did! If you didn't know about Barone's intention to give us damning information on DHS tactics, it wouldn't be so clear. But we do know!" she said emphatically.

"OK, OK. Now that you have it figured, I expect you'll call R.J. and find out what's going on with Wade," said Mac.

"You're smarter than you sound sometimes. Yes, I'll call R.J. because Wade and Roberts are the only two of the three left alive. I'll ask

R.J. for a rundown on both Roberts and Wade. Maybe we'll pick up on some inside chatter on what they think happened to Roberts, as well as Wade's current situation. Do you want me to go through Chancellor in New Zealand as before or go direct?" she asked.

"For the time being, we should go through Chancellor. That way there is no direct link to us regarding any inquiries about Roberts or Wade," Mac said.

Life in Reno was wearing thin, because Mac and Sarah kept a low profile. They were observing with some interest the progress of the tax changes nationally. The former local senator in Nevada had for years been at the top of the sale of tax and other benefits scams for his own profit. He seems to have retired well.

The reports started coming in and the first was from Steel.

"We're getting the slow walk again from the feds," said Steel. "They're even going back to the idea that it was Uncle Bob's fault that he got shot by some hero DHS agents. I think they'll make a deal of some sort, but they are definitely pulling back from where they were. We may have to intensify our lawsuit to move this along."

"Do it," said Mac.

The next report was from R.J. through Robert Chancellor:

"Roberts is missing and Wade is back in the States. Since Wade apparently no longer works for anyone that we can find out about, it suggests that he might be working for the DHS in an 'off the books' capacity. It would not be a stretch to take that a step further to conclude Wade is an assassin. None of our sources on the inside of any agency believes that Barone voluntarily overdosed. His former connection to Wade cannot be ignored.

"You asked us to check out three people; Roberts, Wade and Barone. Roberts is missing and possibly on the run. Wade finished up his job in Nigeria and is back in the States, and Barone is definitely dead – probably murdered. We have not been able to track Wade. He is perhaps on the hunt or maybe hiding," concluded R.J.'s report.

"This report from R.J. makes me think we are the next targets of Wade," said Sarah.

"That's not good news," replied Mac.

"On the contrary, he probably can't find us, since we're under the radar. If we want to find him, all we need to do is surface somewhere and he'll come to us. I say game on! We pick the place and he goes down," she said.

"Just like that?" asked Mac.

"Well, maybe there's a bit more to it than that, but you get the main idea," she said.

# Chapter 19

Nearly a month had gone by since Wade had dispatched Barone. It was time to move along to the next assignment. First, Wade needed to find Macdonald. Wade's last report of a Mac sighting was several months ago at Macdonald's condo in Los Angeles. DHS had nothing more recent. Clearly Macdonald has dropped out of sight, but Wade wondered why.

It was both surprising and alarming to Cecilia Carlson to hear from Wade. She recalled his last visit to her office before the election, when he and Roberts conducted a bogus raid to discourage her opposition to the income tax.

She let the call go to voicemail instead of answering the phone.

"This is former agent Wade; perhaps you remember my visit some time ago. I'm calling because I would like to contact Gordon Macdonald and I thought you might be able to help. I have some information I know he would be interested in. I'll leave my contact number and hope to hear back from you. My number is ..."

Former agent Wade was about the last person on Earth that Cecilia Carlson was interested in speaking with. "I wonder if his call is a ruse to get me to lead him to Macdonald?" she wondered out loud.

From her contacts with the committee just after the election and when the effort to eliminate the income tax was in limbo, she was aware of the killing of Robert Macdonald and the departure of Gordon Macdonald from any visible activity. She also knew first-hand what a thug Wade was.

Secure communications were a necessary element in most personal, legal and financial matters. Government snooping is bad enough, but private hackers were listening in too!

The Lindbergh, Carlson and Jones Law Firm had such a system that did not permit the destination or the content of the calls to be discovered.

Cecilia placed a call to Maggie with the expectation that the information about Wade would reach Mac.

The call from Maggie came early Saturday morning. Mac picked up the phone and Maggie said, "Hi Mac, there is some news about one of the former DHS agents that was involved in harassing our associates early on in the campaign."

Mac asked, "Which agent and who reported the news?"

"You may remember the Lindberg, Carlson and Jones Law Firm in Minneapolis that was raided by two DHS agents; Roberts and Wade. It seems that Wade is fishing around trying to get a location on you. His line is that he has some information for you," said Maggie.

"I'll bet he does," said Mac. "Did Cecilia Carlson contact you?"

"Yes, Mac. She asked me if there is any response she should make to Wade," said Maggie.

"I don't know. Let me talk to Sarah about it and I'll get back to you," said Mac.

Sarah was exulted. "The contact from Wade is just what the doctor ordered," she said.

"How so?" asked Mac.

"Here is a shot at giving Wade a location we choose without his realizing why we want him there," she answered.

"Carlson gives him clues and he figures something out?" asked Mac.

"Maybe, although just using a non-secure phone line would be enough. You know Wade has the capacity to listen in and trace the call," said Sarah.

"We could lead him around for a while. Then set up our own

ambush site," he said.

"Where should we start out? What location?" she asked.

"Let's get him to Reno. We could get a cell phone with that as a billing address, call Carlson's law firm on the non-secure line and Wade will come a calling. Before he can get there, we abandon the Reno apartment and move to a spot that will favor us. We use the same cell phone so he can track our new location," he said.

"I'll set it up with Carlson. But first we let her know by way of a secure line what's going on. Then we'll be calling her back again on an unsecured line, fully aware that the new call can be traced. This will take about a week or so to organize," said Sarah.

"It will take time to create a plan for Wade," said Mac, "We need more firepower. He isn't a poorly functioning clown like Roberts.

"Our only advantage is that he most likely doesn't realize we intend to kill him. As far as he knows, we are the target and he is the hunter.

"His MO is forced entry and for that he may need help. He might just try and sneak in. For sure he'll case our residence. The two places we have don't favor us. He can just bide his time, commit the deed and escape. The local police will never find out who the killer was – that's probably how Barone met his end.

"What we need is a more remote location where we live and can control and observe access," said Mac.

"I see where you're going with this," said Sarah. "We get Vacation Partners into the act; acquire a rural acreage property further north and set up for action."

As they drove north to the Vacation Partners' property, they passed by several small rural towns and it brought to mind the Ruby Ridge incident that Mac remembered all too well.

"By the way," Mac said, "We just passed by Naples, which is the town near Ruby Ridge, where the government killing occurred back in 1992.

"Well, old man, fill me in on that – I was just a child then," said Sarah.

"True, you were in high school, where that event was not a big concern. It's kind of a long story, but I'll give you an executive summary. The incident ended with a confrontation between Randy Weaver, who is a low-profile citizen trying to live with his family off the grid and the U.S. Marshals Service and the FBI. There were three fatalities: Weaver's son, his wife, and on the other side, a U.S. marshal.

"Weaver had associated with some fringe political and social individuals and as a result became ensnarled in an ATF enforcement action. Weaver was falsely alleged to have committed firearms violations. He was also accused of conspiracy against the government and bank robbery. It was all a frame-up on the part of the government. Not only was Weaver acquitted of all charges, but he and his daughters won a multi-million dollar award for the wrongful deaths of their family members.

"Even with that verdict and weeks of congressional hearings, the U.S. government agencies involved never admitted to wrongdoing. To this day, our government seems out of control," concluded Mac.


Their road trip took just a few hours and quickly revealed the perfect environment for the plan; quiet and sparsely populated, the log cabin-style house owned by Vacation Partners was situated on a 20-acre parcel just south of Bonners Ferry, Idaho.

They met with the real estate agent and Mac introduced himself and Sarah as writing contributors to travel guides commissioned by Vacation Partners, which held title to the property. That seemed to satisfy any curiosity the real estate agent may have had and he led the way along the gravel driveway some 100 yards from the road, up a gentle rise to the clearing where the log cabin was located, handed Mac the keys, and gracefully departed.

As they explored the cabin, Sarah noted the security system

amounted to only a burglar alarm and nothing else. "Mac, we must get a security and surveillance system in here. I can have South Bay set it up using Vacation Partners as the client," said Sarah.

"I agree, but even with that, we may be overmatched by Wade," said Mac.

"Mac, I've hesitated to bring this up, but maybe we should contact my brother, Cliff. He might be able to help us, but then again, I worry that it wouldn't be fair to him. After all this isn't his fight," said Sarah.

"No it really isn't. Uncle Bob wasn't his relative," said Mac.

"True, but I am, and I know he'd do anything to help me," said Sarah.

"What could we offer to Cliff as an exit plan if this battle goes the wrong way? Even if we succeed at first, there is the danger of future conflict. I don't think he wants to live his life looking over his shoulder," said Mac.

"That's our issue as well. What are we going to do?" asked Sarah.

"It depends on what happens," said Mac. "If we succeed in killing Wade, and leaving no trace, we have a chance. The problem is, if Wade doesn't return from his mission, whoever sent him will suspect we took him out and might try again. Even if we make it look like an accident, they might still pursue it. Although without proof, maybe not, the whole reason they're trying to kill me now is because I'm pursuing the case against the government for murdering Uncle Bob. They don't want the truth to come out," said Mac.

"What if we kill Wade and then agree to a confidential settlement on the Uncle Bob matter? Hopefully before they get another agent on the way looking for us," said Sarah.

"That might work, but what if they don't live up to their agreement? After all, honesty is not their long suit. I could see leaving the country for a while. Maybe permanently," said Mac.

"We could offer Cliff a new life in New Zealand, if he wants to join up," said Sarah.

"We should minimize any traceable public contact with Cliff if he does decide to help us. Maybe you should pay him a visit by yourself and sound him out on the idea," said Mac.

"Good idea, I'll do it," said Sarah.

"While you're contacting Cliff, I'll respond to Cecilia about calling Wade. We need about a month to set this plan up. Maybe we should forget about having Reno as the first stop. This will be the best and only location," said Mac.

The security system was installed and although nothing special, it had all the basics that an insurance underwriter would ask for: a few motion sensors, with cameras outside and a monitor inside.

Sarah returned from her visit with Cliff bearing good news: he was in.

Mac felt suddenly relieved. "I know we're the ones with the motivation, but I always wondered if we have the actual skills to finish the job. I think this Wade person will be difficult.

"What did Cliff say?" asked Mac.

"We had quite an extended conversation – at least by Cliff's standards. After some catch-up on our lives, I went into the tax project and the resulting murder of Uncle Bob. To him, there is no doubt that retribution is called for.

"His impression of the private security forces, like Wade, in Iraq is mixed. Some good, some bad. He did say that we should be able to take care of business. On the subject of what happens after Wade, he was uncertain. I got the feeling he might be considering a change of course in his life though," said Sarah.

# Chapter 20

Wade was close to giving up on hearing back from Cecilia Carlson. It had been a month since he had contacted her regarding Gordon Macdonald. No trace of his query had turned up anywhere.

Then the message came in from Carlson, giving a cell phone number for Mac. Wade had no intention of calling the number until Macdonald was located. It had a 208 area code, which meant it was in Idaho. Wade would start there first.

Mac accelerated the process. He called Wade on the callback number he received from Carlson.

"Wade, this is Macdonald calling. I understand you wish to contact me regarding my uncle's killing," said Mac.

"Yes, I do, Mr. Macdonald. First I want to say I am personally sorry and that it was an accident," said Wade.

"True or not, that doesn't do me any good. Is that all you have to say? Because if it is, I'm not interested," said Mac.

"There is something else. I'd like to meet with you personally, because this involves sensitive material," said Wade.

"I'll bet it does. If you want to tell me my uncle died because the government, or parts thereof, was going to stop the tax protest at any cost, than you can save your breath. I already know that. As far as I'm concerned, you can go to hell. Don't bother me again," said Mac as he hung up the phone.

As that conversation went, it served both sides. Wade was able to contact, and through a phone trace locate, Macdonald. And Mac had baited the trap.

"I hope we know what we're doing," said Sarah after listening to the recording of the Wade phone call.

"When will Cliff be here? We need his help now," said Mac.

"He's on his way. Should arrive early in the evening today," replied Sarah.

As expected, Cliff appeared, driving the customary Ram pickup. It was probably painted some shade of gray underneath the layers of mountain West dust and dirt. Unloading it was revealing, in that there was combat equipment for long range, intermediate and close up. Also, not to be ignored, was the archery gear. The pickup was put away out of sight and the planning began.

Cliff stood about 6-foot-2 and was an imposing figure. At 35 years old, he is physically fit like the outdoor hunter type he is.

"Cliff, it's great to see you here," said Mac. "I don't know how much Sarah has told you of our situation, but for sure we could use your help."

"I've got the basic story. I'm sorry to hear about your Uncle, Mac. It's been several years since I got out of the Marines – a lifetime ago, it seems. Since then, I've been involved in game hunting, both on my own and as a guide for an outfitter. What is your weapons experience, Mac?" asked Cliff.

"Both Sarah and I have some self-defense training with handguns. Also I have hunted a dozen or so times over the past 12 to 15 years. No military training though," said Mac.

"We should move quickly on a defensive plan then. First thing to-morrow, we'll set up for action," said Cliff.


Wade was understandably encouraged at contacting Macdonald, but couldn't help but wonder why he was in North Idaho. Was the contact contrived; a little too easy? he questioned.

After arriving at the Spokane airport in Washington, Wade was on his way to Bonners Ferry, Idaho, which was nearly to the Canadian border.

Macdonald's place was a bit off the beaten track – about six miles east of Highway U.S. 95, just south of town. Few neighbors and none close by. It seemed to be a perfect setup for a sniper attack. After a couple of drive-bys and a walk, in what seemed like an adjacent property, Wade spotted Mac and decided on a plan. He would need some items for his operation first though - something to force the occupants to flee the house into the open where they could be picked off. Flash grenades and smoke bombs would do the job nicely.

Before anything else, Wade needed to confirm Macdonald's routine along with his girlfriend who were living in the house. He decided on a wireless surveillance camera to be set on a utility pole across the street with its view range on the driveway, but not as far as the house. Wade knew he would need a helper on this job.


"There are two ways they can approach us; a sniper attack from some distance, or a home invasion type of strike," said Cliff. "First, we should check the view range of our cameras so that vantage points from which a sniper could operate are covered. Second, we need electronic trip wires that will tell us if there is someone approaching near the house."

"Speaking of cameras, I reviewed this morning's view of the street and I think it shows somebody is already here," said Sarah. "A car went by several times and a man is seen traversing the eastern property line. I think we're coming up on an event."

"What's your best vantage point to oppose a sniper?" asked Mac.

"I don't know for sure. There's the barn with a loft which has a decent field of vision. Also, there are some trees with dense undergrowth that might work for a ground level position along the side yards. I don't have to stay in one place," said Cliff.

"From now on, we need one of us to check on the monitor frequently and another to be outside in a shooting position at least at night," said Mac. "We can each work four three or four hour shifts a day with an hour between shifts. That way we each work 15 to 16 hours a day. At least one of us, either Cliff or I, will be outside 24 hours a day. The days are getting shorter now. It's dark at six in the evening and the sun comes up about six in the morning. We have about 12 hours of darkness to cover," said Mac.

Wade had kept track of Roberts for just such a situation as this. Roberts was at loose ends because of the deposition demand and eager to resolve the matter in the usual way - to just kill someone.

Wade funded the acquisition of rifles, flash grenades, smoke bombs and some surveillance gear. It was good to team up with Roberts once again, thought Wade.

"Let's take a drive-by of Macdonald's place so you can get the lay of the land," said Wade.

"How about first thing, say about 6:30 tomorrow morning?" replied Roberts.

As they drove by, Sarah caught them on the monitor. Cliff was in the loft of the barn and Sarah alerted him. They made two passes and Cliff realized it was Wade with a companion. "If they are impatient, they'll be back tonight. Or maybe they'll just make more observations first."

It was later that afternoon when an unmarked van showed up and stopped in front of the utility pole across the street. Sarah saw it on the monitor and alerted Mac, who was in the loft. Mac had the telescope and could see the serviceman climb the pole and attach an object just above the crossarm on the pole. As the serviceman descended the pole, Mac sauntered from the house along the driveway to the mailbox located on the street near the pole. The serviceman gave a friendly wave and departed. Mac had helped the identification process along. Wade now knew for sure where his quarry was.

Cliff had been asleep and Sarah woke him up to report what she and Mac had observed. Cliff went to a vantage point at one of the second-story dormer windows and found the object with his telescope. Looks like a surveillance camera, he thought.

The three discussed their options and decided to take it out. One shot from Cliff and it was gone.

"Will they react to their missing camera with another visit? Or just come hunting regardless?" asked Mac.

"I think they'll come tonight. Their camera wasn't an essential part of the plan. I can set up outside where they'll have to pass by me," said Cliff.

"We'll shift the monitor for our cameras to the barn. It'll be safer there for Sarah to keep track of the situation. Both Cliff and I will be outside looking to take preemptive shots," said Mac.


Wade and Roberts realized their camera was out of commission, but did not concern themselves over it. They were ready to go regardless.

"We'll strike at 3 a.m. so we'll have time to finish and leave the area before dawn. It'll take seven or eight minutes to drive from the scene to U.S. 95. If we use the flash grenades and smoke bombs, it'll take maybe four or five minutes for Macdonald and whoever else is in the house to evacuate and go outside. Another three minutes to make sure the job is done, then we should be back on U.S. 95 inside of twenty minutes from start to finish," said Wade.

Wade and Roberts had proceeded 25 yards or so on foot from their car, carrying the explosives. Roberts would be the one to fire the grenades and smoke bombs and Wade would be the shooter.

Cliff knew they were there. From his vantage point on the side yard near the street, he could see the two separate to perform their individual tasks.

Roberts was the closest to Cliff and was preparing to launch the smoke bomb and flash grenade. An arrow silently found its mark between Roberts' shoulder blades and that job was done – Roberts never knew what hit him.

Wade never heard a thing so he didn't know Roberts was dead. He was positioned on the side of the driveway to take his shot when the occupants of the house would appear as a result of the coming blast – which never came. He unknowingly had set off a trip wire. Now everyone knew he was there.

Cliff was first to gain a shooting position with his night vision gear. A single shot took Wade down.

Cliff gave Mac and Sarah the all-clear and then they congregated to clean up the scene. Wade's body was placed in the trunk, Roberts's in the front seat and all the gear they brought in the rear seat of their car.

The Kootenai River, about a 30-mile drive just into Montana, was notable for its 200 to 250-foot canyon walls overlooking the river. It was there, several days later, at the foot of the precipice, that recently deceased Wade and Roberts, along with their belongings, would be found in the wreck of their car. It happened in the dark, and bad weather had provided cover for days and there was no witness report at or near the time of the event.

To the Montana State Patrol, the scene looked like a mob hit. Who else would stuff a body shot dead into a trunk of a car and push it over a cliff? And was the guy in the front seat a perpetrator or victim? Maybe the FBI should figure this out.

It had been a dreary winter in Idaho, but the sun always seems to shine in Southern California - even in January. Dugan was the first to make contact upon the return of Mac, Sarah and Cliff to L.A. "Would Mac and Sarah be interested in the latest chapter in the IRS saga?" inquired Dugan.

Sarah retrieved the message from South Bay Security and asked Mac, "What do you suppose Dugan has here?"

The meeting convened at the Yacht Club in Marina Del Rey with Dugan, Mac, Sarah and Cliff. Dugan did not disappoint. His sources within the IRS had brought to light the reason for commissioner Barton's death.

"Barton was a highly regarded guy in D.C.," Dugan explained. "He was doing the administration a favor by taking the IRS job because the government needed credibility. As he got into the requests and demands from Congress for data on IRS operations, he became uneasy about something even worse. Barton began to suspect the IRS was the financial manager and one of the enforcers for a massive government shake-down scheme."

Mac interrupted. "We found out early on in our tax reform effort that the IRS and other elements of the government had been corrupted and to me it explained Uncle Bob's murder by federal agents," he said. "Those involved in the government racket knew that the investigation of the IRS would doom their extracurricular activities."

Dugan continued. "You are right on that. The shake-down program is at or coming to an end. There is, however, an interesting loose end.

There is quite a substantial sum of money that has been collected from the victims, but not yet disbursed to the individuals who were managing the shake-down activities."

"Do you know where the money is?" asked Sarah.

"I think so. At least I know where it has been and maybe still is," replied Dugan.

"I assume you have a reason for telling us about the shake-down scheme and the money," said Mac.

"I do," replied Dugan.

"What is that reason?" asked Sarah.

"Would you like to get rich? I mean really rich?" asked Dugan. "Let me continue. There's a fund that has operated for years known as the Supplementary Pension Fund. It was set up for senior bureaucratic managers to distribute the shake-down proceeds after expenses to those top and middle level officials and a few government labor union chiefs. In a half-hearted attempt to be discreet, they usually wait until an individual retires to distribute his or her share. It is all done offshore and they get away with it because the IRS is the cop on the beat. It's been going on for years. They use a Panama-based bank and the Panama authorities don't bother with it because the IRS tells them not to; not to mention the fees that the Panama officials earn."

Cliff, who had not spoken up until now, said, "I'm not a banker or businessman, but I think I'm getting the drift of this conversation. We can steal this money. Am I right?"

"I prefer the word 'take' the money. It has already been stolen," said Dugan.

"Why us?" asked Sarah.

"The exact skillset needed is in this room," replied Dugan.

"How so?" asked Mac.

"We need technical skill, planning, physical protection and inside knowledge. I'll leave it to you to connect the dots," replied Dugan.

"Do you have a framework of an agreement in mind?" asked Mac.

"Yes, but first you should discuss the idea and determine your interest in participating or not," said Dugan, "Let's resume our discussion tomorrow."

Later that day, Mac led off: "If we quit now, we have a good chance of reaching some sort of standoff. Our adversaries in the shake-down operation may have bigger problems then continuing to hunt us down. After all, if we continue our legal attack on them for Uncle Bob's murder, that could get messy. They can't prove our involvement in the demise of Roberts or Wade without opening themselves up to discovery of their own criminal behavior."

"Sometimes I wonder about you, Mac," said Sarah.

"They won't go after us - only in a court of law. They will just send someone else to kill us."

"If we can't really quit, why not go for the money?" asked Cliff.

"Dugan didn't come to us for no reason. I think he knows about our involvement with Roberts and Wade," said Sarah.

"Maybe you are right. Their party at the IRS and the DHS may be coming to an end. It may be possible to outlast them, particularly if we have resources. Let's hear Dugan out," said Mac.

"Dugan is turning out to be quite the master of intrigue," said Sarah. "If he knows or thinks we killed Roberts and Wade and if he knows the shake-down payment plan and who gets the money, he can have something on everyone. His only challenge is to capitalize on that knowledge without getting killed in the process. Are we supposed to be his protection?"

"I never thought I would wind up being a gunslinger for a former IRS clerk," said Mac.

The meeting began the following day in Dugan's hotel room. He knew it was clean as far as listening devices were concerned. The invited guests were likewise checked for such listening items. Mac, Sarah and Cliff took the inspection in stride, because at least it showed Dugan to be a careful man.

Cliff got into the spirit and used Dugan's detection equipment to determine if Dugan himself was clean. He was and so the conversation began.

"How would it strike you if I told you that there is a large sum of money that was illegally extorted from businesses and individuals in exchange for exceptions to certain federal regulations that at this moment is up for grabs?" asked Dugan.

"I would be interested," said Mac, with Sarah and Cliff both nodding their assent.

"I will begin by expressing what I believe to be a necessary understanding between the four of us. Mac, as you know, your uncle and I had some dealings over many years and had developed a mutual trust – likewise with you.

"I've been able to work with Sarah at South Bay Security enough to also develop a trust. With respect to Cliff, I will accept your vouching for him. Let me ask how you feel about working with me on what is no doubt a dangerous endeavor," said Dugan.

"That's a tall order to deal with right off the bat. We would need more information on the endeavor, as you put it, to assess the level of risk," said Mac.

"That's OK with me and if you agree, that what I am about to tell you is absolutely confidential, I will proceed," said Dugan.

"Agreed," Mac, Sarah and Cliff responded.

"Some two decades ago, a shadow federal government organization took form to consolidate and systemize the erratic pattern of petty graft that had been going on pretty much forever. Several levels of government employees take part from nearly every department and bureau. The highest level person ever caught was the vice president in the mid-1970s, who was discovered to have solicited and accepted cash bribes while governor of a state prior to being elected vice president of the United States.

"The senior management for the shadow organization comes from the DOJ and the IRS. Also helpful are the folks from DHS.

"The system works like this: The bribes are paid mainly in cash to a government contact who gets 10 percent off the top, up to $10,000 per deal, and passes the rest to a consolidator in the IRS. The IRS manages what is fondly called the Supplemental Pension Fund. The fund has bank accounts to launder the money and make payments to plan members when they depart the government. The DOJ supervises and assists the IRS in their management of the Supplemental Pension Fund," said Dugan.

"How do they get a bank to do the money management? That's clearly illegal! What kind of a bank does that?" asked Mac.

"They didn't have to look very far," replied Dugan, "The CIA had such a bank during the Cold War. It was the Bank of Credit and Commerce International, or BCCI, domiciled in a foreign country with a weak supervisory agency. The BCCI did what it was instructed to do and the bank regulators were paid off to cooperate. No objection from the U.S. government was made until after the end of the Cold War. That, unsurprisingly, is when the BCCI ended. Hardly anyone has heard of the bank now used. It is called International Payment Systems or IPS. The bank never gets caught because the DOJ and IRS don't want that to happen," said Dugan.

"What do you think makes it possible to attack the group, their plan and their bank at this time?" asked Sarah.

"Simple, really. The exposure of the IRS means the shadow group has lost its main operational element. Who could fill in? The DOJ can manipulate the law, but they can't strong-arm enough businesses and individuals to keep the racket going. They are going to shut down and there is $220 million of undisbursed funds," said Dugan.

"Assuming you have an idea of how to access the money, we come into the picture to facilitate the movement and thereby the new destination of the fund. Is that about it?" asked Sarah.

"Yes," replied Dugan.

"Give us a day or two, so we can consider our involvement. It is a long-term proposition," said Mac.

"Of course. You should know up front that I want half, after expenses," said Dugan.

Chapter 21

"Sarah, would you have South Bay make sure Uncle Bob's place is not bugged?" asked Mac. "It's livable and it's going to take some time to sell it anyway. We might as well set up there."

Over the next few days, everything considered, Mac, Sarah and Cliff decided to join in with Dugan. It would possibly mean leaving the U.S. for some time. Mac and Sarah had considered such a move before and Cliff could deal with that idea, too.

Dugan laid out the plan: One of his acquaintances at the IRS, until now unbeknownst to Dugan, was involved with the pension plan. He was discreetly looking for help to control the fund. Inspector West contacted Dugan.

"I have been speaking with Jason West for a month and he wants me to help him keep control of the fund. I think he was involved with the killing of the IRS Commissioner Barton.

"He thinks I can help because I'm retired and would not be under the same level of observation that he would as a current employee. By the way, he has been involved with the late Mr. Barone in the course of their business," said Dugan.

"Did he have anything to do with Uncle Bob's murder?" asked Mac.

"Maybe. He and a DOJ lawyer named Foster had operational control of intimidation activities," answered Dugan.

"What is West's intention for disposition of the pension fund?" asked Sarah.

"I think he will want to take some himself, pay some out to other senior participants in the group who could be a problem if they were left out," said Dugan.

"What does that leave the four of us, according to the West plan?" asked Sarah.

"We are sort of outside contractors and our payment would be considered as an overhead cost of doing business. Maybe ten percent, plus expenses," said Dugan.

"What do you think of that plan?" asked Sarah.

"It's a great plan for West and his friends, but I have another plan," said Dugan. "We play along for a while to get access to the fund and then we take it all! In the process, we spin some money out to the group; just enough to incriminate them in the scheme, which is bound to come to light at some point."

"Will West and the DOJ lawyer know who else is involved besides you?" asked Sarah.

"Probably not, if that is the way you want it," said Dugan.

"What do you think West will do when he figures out we took the money?" asked Sarah.

"He can't go public or use his customary IRS or DOJ muscle without incriminating himself. So what he has left is off the record types like Roberts and Wade to fight back. By the way, have you heard Barone and Wade are dead and Roberts is M.I.A. and possibly dead?" said Dugan.

"No kidding!" said Mac, who had been quiet since West and Foster had come up as likely involved in Uncle Bob's murder. For Mac, this caper was now about much more than the money.

# Chapter 23

West of the IRS and Foster of the DOJ had frequent and urgent meetings. The end was near and they both knew it. It was proving difficult for both of them to plan and act without relying on the coercive power they had wielded as government agents.

"I have contacted a former IRS agent named Dugan to help us with the disbursement and dissolution of the Supplemental Pension Fund," said West.

"Why this guy?" asked Foster.

"He's a retired long-term IRS agent. I knew him for years and I think he is capable, but just corrupt enough to take some money, count himself lucky and go away," said West.

"Who else would be involved?" asked Foster.

"I don't know. that will be up to Dugan," said West. "His interest is to manage this well and so I think he will. It's best that the knowledge of who all is involved be limited."

"OK, so what's the plan?" asked Foster.

"I'll have Dugan set up offshore accounts in partnership names, newly created for you, me, 40 of our associates, and Dugan. The accounts will be in branches of international banks we have used in the past, including and beginning with International Payment Systems, where the money is. As you know, the IPS is headquartered in Panama with a dozen branches in other places.

"Once each recipient is notified of the receipt of his funds, he shall transfer the money to other accounts with other vesting so as to make the tracing difficult.

"To start the plan in motion, once the receiving accounts are set up, it requires two authorizations to start the money moving from where it is. Those two authorizations are yours and mine. They are codes, not names, so as to not be easily traced. The vesting on the existing account is 1776 Partners. From here on, we will be independent.

"I have prepared a schedule of amounts each recipient will receive for your review," said West.


Dugan briefed Mac, Sarah and Cliff on the plan that West had devised, including the amounts for each participant.

"I see my role here – we need to tap into their record system and bend it to our will," said Sarah.

"When you have a plan for us, we'll need our own set of accounts to receive and then wire out the funds. The money needs to be split up into smaller, less noteworthy sums," said Dugan.

A week into her efforts, Sarah had succeeded in penetrating the IPS data center.

"I can change their numbers when the money is to be transferred," reported Sarah.

"In order to make everything seem normal for a while, should we allow everyone on the list to receive a little something?" asked Dugan.

"I can move the decimal point one place to the left and for Dugan's share, the decimal will move one place to the right," said Sarah.

"How does that add up for the distribution of the $220 million?" asked Dugan.

"I have thought about various strategies and I believe we must depend on deception at the beginning. The longer Foster and West don't realize that tampering has occurred, the farther away we can transfer and obscure the trail of our money," said Sarah.

"Do we leave the Foster and West shares as they are?" asked Mac.

"Yes, because if we shift the decimal point to the left for the 40 other individuals and to the right for Dugan, it would mean that Foster would get his expected $22 million, West his expected $22, million, the 40 others will get $400,000 each for a total of $16 million, and Dugan $154 million. If we allow $6 million for expenses and split 50-50, it means you, Mr. Dugan, get $75 million and we get $75 million or about $25 million each for Mac, Cliff and me," said Sarah.

"If we pull this off, as you describe, there will be 40 individuals who will quickly realize they have been screwed and then they will look to West and Foster, who in turn will go after me!" said Dugan.

"That risk is why you got a larger share," said Mac.

"I know, but in order to survive, I need some help and that is part of why I brought you in," said Dugan.

"We all need a plan. Let's work on some ideas and meet tomorrow," said Mac.

Dugan left and the discussion with Mac, Sarah and Cliff continued.

"Mac, you have been rather quiet during this whole planning process and now you come to life. Why?" asked Sarah.

"For me, this whole project has been about retribution for my uncle's murder. West and Foster are the final pieces. I'm going after them both. Our lawyer Ron Steel, with our lawsuit, will be the route we take," said Mac.

"They find us!" corrected Cliff and Sarah nodded assent.

"How do you see the money path going for West and Foster?" asked Mac.

"The first stop for them and Dugan is Panama with a loosely affiliated Panamanian bank that enjoys generous fees connected to this trade. The IRS and CIA have used them for decades. Dugan's first transfer will land there in two different accounts. The banker will no doubt be surprised at the amount for Dugan. We will pay the banker off. From there, it will be split into a half dozen more accounts with different vestings in still more locations," said Sarah.

"Do Dugan or the others ever have to appear in person while all this transferring goes on?" asked Mac.

"Not until the recipient needs the money for his use," said Sarah. "Then he needs to set up credit cards and transaction accounts. He can do these things or have a lawyer do it. But at some point he has to be near the process."

"I don't think West and Foster are going to be that patient," replied Mac. "When they see how much Dugan is getting, they – or someone they send – may get in touch with the Panamanian banker in order to stop the transaction and recover the money," said Mac.

"Someone would have to appear in person with evidence of authority at the bank in order to change things around. Our new friend, the banker, will not reverse the transaction otherwise. By the time someone makes that contact, Dugan's money should be on its way. By the way, where do we have our share sent?" asked Sarah.

"There is a trust that I control in New Zealand that owns a shell bank in Nauru. I bought it in 2005 for almost nothing after the Nauru government passed anti-tax haven laws under pressure from the Intergovernmental Task Force on Money Laundering. The reason to use that bank as a pass-through is that even if the transaction is reported and discovered, the true ownership of the money, once it is sent on to several multi-level trusts I have had for years, will remain confidential. I can deposit and access the money in several Asian and South Pacific jurisdictions."

The expatriate community in Baja California is alive and well. For decades, the Americans have settled in, both full and part time. Anything you need can be bought - nice accommodations and other creature comforts, including personal security. Dugan picked Cabo for his retirement nest.

Dugan did not pick Mexico for his major banking needs. He picked Liechtenstein, the gold standard for asset protection. The fees are a bit high, but nobody takes your money away. All you need to make that work is plenty of money and a good lawyer. Dugan had both.

Payday was drawing close. A clandestine meeting at a roadside motel just south of D.C. was attended by Foster, West and Dugan.

Dugan reported, "I've set up accounts in Panama, Aruba and Cayman for the 40 individuals you have designated. For you two, I split it up between the Isle of Man, Guernsey, Hong Kong and for a nice touch, Dubai. The idea behind those selections is that the banks won't fail and confidentiality is their game."

Payday came and went without incident. The $220 million in the Supplementary Pension Fund  was disbursed. It was the next two days when it hit the fan. The 40 recipients on the short end of the stick were calling West.

It didn't take too long to realize Dugan had stuck it to the group. The record of disbursements confirmed that. West's first efforts to reach Dugan failed.

Another day passed and the pressure was building - then Dugan called West, much to West's surprise.

"We have been hacked!" said Dugan.

"Looks like you did it," replied West.

"I have an idea to discuss with you. Can we meet? I can come over to your residence tonight," said Dugan.

"This better be good, Dugan – so far you're not looking too good. Be here at nine sharp," said West.

West called Foster, "Dugan called and wants to meet at my place tonight. Do you think I should meet with him? And would you like to attend?"

"Yes, let's meet with him – he's got a lot of explaining to do," re-plied Foster. "I'll bring along one of my security people just in case."

Dugan arrived at West's residence as agreed. He carried a

briefcase which was promptly grabbed and searched by the security person. What was found in the briefcase was an envelope containing documents.

"What do we have here?" asked West.

"This is your ticket to prison if these documents become known to the FBI," said Dugan.

Taken aback, West asked, "What the hell are you talking about? We're all in this together!"

"Not really, there's no record of my involvement. However, there is a long record of your involvement. An executive summary of chapter and verse of your involvement is here for your perusal. Other copies will remain secure as long as I am not harmed in any way. It should be very clear to you that you should take your payout, which was purposely left intact, disappear and shut up. You might also be well advised to recommend to the others that they do likewise," said Dugan.

The story was brief; three column inches below the fold on page three of the Honolulu morning paper. Sarah noticed it while she and Mac were enjoying their morning coffee on the lanai of their room overlooking the beach.

"According to that report, it seems that a workplace violence event occurred in connection with the retirement party for a long-term IRS official by the name of Jason West. The investigation is ongoing, but the preliminary belief is that the shooter was a co-worker who expressed anger with Inspector West over some sort of unmet obligation. Then the alleged perpetrator was in turn shot dead by the police."

Sarah related the news article to Mac, who paused and then he remarked, "When Ben Franklin was writing some 220 years ago, he observed that nothing can be said to be certain, except death and taxes. Today he would likely note that there is a causal connection between the two."

# Acknowledgements

To a great extent this book comes from a family effort. My wife, Ursula helped me throughout the writing with thoughtful observations. Daughter, Elizabeth got me started on the right track with her writing expertise.

Thanks also to Dorothy Eldridge my transcriber and to the staff of Keokee Publishing who capably managed the production of this book.

www.ingramcontent.com/pod-product-compliance
Lightning Source LLC
Chambersburg PA
CBHW030353180626
46812CB00007B/2871